"Thanks for inviting me to stay."

"You're good company," she said.

"So are you." Their eyes met and she felt a tingle down to her toes. The sensation surprised her. It made her a little nervous. But it also made her hopeful. Not all of her had died with Jonas.

He insisted on helping clean the dishes, and she thought she might ask him to stay a little longer, for coffee or a glass of wine. Would she ask him to stay the night? Too soon, she thought, but she enjoyed contemplating the idea.

It didn't make her nearly as nervous as she thought such a big step would. Maybe that was because at least part of her was ready to move on to a future without Jonas. Yes, he had been gone two years, but he was still such a huge, important part of her life. Maybe she was working toward letting him go so they could both rest in peace.

D0381414

PURSUIT AT PANTHER POINT

CINDI MYERS

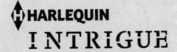

HARLEQUIN

INTRIGUE

For Lucy

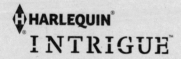

ISBN-13: 978-1-335-59116-6

Pursuit at Panther Point

Copyright © 2023 by Cynthia Myers

Recycling programs
for this product may
not exist in your area.

For questions and comments about the quality of this book,
please contact us at CustomerService@Harlequin.com.

Harlequin Enterprises ULC
22 Adelaide St. West, 41st Floor
Toronto, Ontario M5H 4E3, Canada
www.Harlequin.com

Printed in U.S.A.

Cindi Myers is the author of more than seventy-five novels. When she's not plotting new romance story lines, she enjoys skiing, gardening, cooking, crafting and daydreaming. A lover of small-town life, she lives with her husband and two spoiled dogs in the Colorado mountains.

Books by Cindi Myers

Harlequin Intrigue

Eagle Mountain: Critical Response

Deception at Dixon Pass
Pursuit at Panther Point

Eagle Mountain Search and Rescue

Eagle Mountain Cliffhanger
Canyon Kidnapping
Mountain Terror
Close Call in Colorado

Eagle Mountain: Search for Suspects

Disappearance at Dakota Ridge
Conspiracy in the Rockies
Missing at Full Moon Mine
Grizzly Creek Standoff

The Ranger Brigade: Rocky Mountain Manhunt

Investigation in Black Canyon
Mountain of Evidence
Mountain Investigation
Presumed Deadly

Visit the Author Profile page at Harlequin.com.

CAST OF CHARACTERS

Deputy Lucas Malone—On temporary assignment in Eagle Mountain, Lucas is surprised to find himself embroiled in a murder investigation and once again linked with Anna Trent, a woman he met two years previous while both their partners were dying of cancer.

Anna Trent—Anna is embarrassed to see Lucas again and is sure he must think badly of her, so her attraction to the deputy surprises her. Determined to find answers to her friend's shocking death, she keeps meeting up with Lucas, and as she does, the attraction grows.

Dave Weiss—The popular bakery owner appears to have hanged himself, but those closest to him, including Anna, believe his death may have been caused by someone else.

Sandy Weiss—A former bodybuilder and volunteer firefighter, Sandy has always been dismissive of Anna. But she was devoted to Dave and appears to be working hard to rebuild her life after his death.

George Anders—George has a business linking small providers like Dave with restaurants in the area who want to feature local products. He lent Dave a lot of money to help him expand the business and has recently been linked to a drug-distribution ring operating through local restaurants.

Chapter One

Anna Trent had been drawn to search and rescue work because she wanted to help people. But sometimes, like today, helping hurt more than she had bargained for.

"I'm sorry to have to ask you to do this, but he's been missing more than twenty-four hours now and Sandy is worried sick. We all are, really." Eagle Mountain Search and Rescue Captain Sheri Stevens rested one hand on Anna's shoulder. The women stood on the side of a snow-packed road in a remote section of the county, a brisk wind sending devils of snow swirling around their feet. "I know Dave is your friend, too."

"He is. I want to find him as much as everyone else." Anna looked down and met the gaze of her search dog, Jacquie. Maybe it was fanciful to think so, but the poodle's brown eyes seemed to reflect Anna's own concern. When word had spread that Dave Weiss, a popular volunteer fireman and owner of a local bakery, hadn't come home the night before last, Anna's first thought was that he had had an ac-

cident while out ice fishing or back-country skiing.
Eagle Mountain Search and Rescue was on standby
to look for him, but in a county comprised mostly of
wilderness area full of ski trails and fishing holes,
there was no logical place to begin.

Anna was a newer member of the SAR team and,
ordinarily, would be grouped with the other rookies
to sweep a designated area. But Jacquie, a three-year-
old standard poodle who had recently been certified
by Search and Rescue Dogs of Colorado, had already
proved valuable in finding other missing persons. As
tense as searches could be, she was glad to be able
to do more to help find her friend.

A few hours earlier, someone had spotted Dave's
pickup truck parked in this out-of-the-way location
designated on some maps as Panther Point. An inch
of snow from last night's storm covered the truck's
windshield and hood, and obscured any footprints he
may have made after he'd parked the vehicle. Had he
met someone here and driven away with them? Anna
looked down at Jacquie. The dog's black curly coat
was flecked with snow, like a sprinkling of powdered
sugar. She stared up at Anna with solemn brown
eyes, as if she sensed that today wasn't merely a
training exercise. "If anyone can find Dave, Jacquie
can," Anna said.

Sheri moved in a little closer, her voice low. "I
have to warn you. When Sandy called about Dave not
coming home, she told the dispatcher she was worried he might have gone somewhere to kill himself."

Anna rocked back on her heels. "Dave? Why?"

She pictured the man who had become one of her first friends after she had moved to Eagle Mountain five years before. Dave was a cheerful, burly blond, who still had a distinct Austrian accent despite two decades in Colorado. She had been a newlywed who'd known no one other than her new husband, Jonas Trent. Dave had been one of Jonas's best friends and he had welcomed Anna with open arms—literally enveloping her in a warm hug the first time they'd met. After Jonas's death, Dave had always been there, to shovel snow or repair a leaky faucet, or buy her a cup of coffee when they ran into each other downtown. In the past six months, they hadn't seen as much of each other. Anna felt more comfortable standing on her own feet and she suspected Dave's wife, Sandy, had been a little jealous of the attention her husband had paid his friend's widow.

"Sandy said he's been worried about money," Sheri said. "Apparently, they've been stretched pretty thin."

That didn't sound like Dave, either. Jonas had always said his friend was one of the smartest men he knew. He had a solid business and the couple didn't live extravagantly. "I guess we never really know what is going on inside people," Anna said. Maybe in the past six months something about Dave's situation had changed.

Sheri patted her shoulder. "It's terrible, but I wanted to warn you that this search might not have the happy outcome we're all hoping for."

Anna took a firmer hold of the long lead clipped to Jacquie's collar. "We'll do our best to find him. Even if the news is the worst, his family and friends deserve to know what happened." She always reminded herself of this when she and Jacquie set out on a search. Not every hunt, or even most of them, ended with good news, but the work they did was still important.

"Thanks." Sheri stepped back and looked toward the Rayford County Sheriff's Department SUV parked at the edge of the Forest Service road. She raised her hand and the door opened; a man with ink-black hair in sheriff's department khakis and a black leather jacket stepped out.

"Who is that?" Anna asked as the deputy started toward them. She thought she knew all the local officers, but this one didn't look familiar. She guessed he was about her age—early thirties—fit and good-looking, at least from what she could see as he walked over, head down.

"He's with the Mesa County Sheriff's Department," Sheri said. "He's filling in while Jamie Douglas is on maternity leave."

"Jamie had her baby?" Anna smiled. The force's only female deputy was a familiar figure around town.

"Two nights ago," Sheri said. "A little girl."

"Hello."

Anna turned her head to the deputy but realized he wasn't addressing her. Instead, he had stopped to pet Jacquie, who vibrated the stub of her tail and leaned into the ear scratch he offered. Smiling, he looked at the women, his eyes meeting Anna's. "Hello," he said again. "Thanks for agreeing to help us."

"Of course." Anna tried to look away, but she couldn't. She didn't know this man's name, but they had definitely met before. A hot flush of embarrassment rose to her cheeks as she remembered their last—and only—encounter. Over two years ago, at the Junction hospital. She had been screaming at a nurse in the corridor, furious that Jonas had been waiting more than an hour for something to relieve the agonizing pain of his end-stage pancreatic cancer. Not her finest moment, made even more embarrassing by the arrival of this officer, who had led her away and persuaded her to calm down.

Was it possible he wouldn't recognize her? After all, she was two years older now, quite a bit calmer and better rested.

"You're looking much better than the last time we met," he said, proving that he hadn't forgotten.

"You didn't see me at my best," she said.

Sheri looked from one to the other. "Do you two know each other?" she asked.

"Not really," Anna said quickly.

"I'm Lucas Malone."

He held out his hand and she took it, his grip firm. "Anna Trent." Had she told him her name that long-ago evening? She couldn't remember.

Sheri looked from one to the other, obviously curious. "We'd better get started," Anna said before her friend could ask any more questions.

"I've never worked with a search dog before," Deputy Malone said. "What do you need from me?"

"Since we're looking for a specific person, it would be good to have something of Dave's for Jacquie to scent," Anna said.

They looked toward the white pickup angled into the brush on the side of the road. "I can probably pop the lock on the truck for you," Malone said.

He returned to his SUV and came back with the tool for jimmying the lock open. While his back was to her as he worked, she studied him. That night at the hospital, she had been too upset for more than his general features to register. Now she noticed the way his leather jacket clung to his broad shoulders, and how the sun glinted on his thick, dark hair. The flutter this awareness sent through her startled her.

He pulled open the door of the truck and turned to her. "Try not to touch anything except the scent item," he said as he stepped back to allow Anna access.

Mind once more on the solemn task ahead, she shoved her right hand into a wrong-side-out plastic bag and leaned into the truck. She scanned the interior, searching for something that might hold Dave's scent. She spotted a can of snuff in the tray on the console. He probably handled that multiple times a day, but she worried the strong mint aroma of the tobacco might dilute his own smells. Jacquie was capable of distinguishing the different scents. Why make things difficult for her?

Instead, she chose a bandana tucked in the tray next to the snuff tin. She picked it up and withdrew her hand from the bag, turning the plastic inside-out as she did so, capturing the bandana neatly in the bag. Jacquie sat, eyes focused on the bag, every muscle tense with anticipation. She knew what came next.

Anna bent and offered the open bag to the dog. Jacquie stuck her nose inside, inhaled deeply, then sampled the ground around the open truck door. Snuffling excitedly, she walked around the truck to the passenger side, sniffed the snowy ground around the truck then turned and dove through a narrow gap in the underbrush alongside the road, tugging hard on the lead.

"Wait here," Sheri called over her shoulder to Malone as she took off after Anna and Jacquie. "I'll radio when we find anything."

Anna's pack slapped against her back as she jogged to keep up with the excited dog. Thirty yards from the road, Jacquie swung right, up an incline, weaving around the white trunks of a thick growth of aspen, bare of leaves this time of year. Anna's boots slipped in the snow and the legs of her pants were already wet from plunging through stands of post oak, dead leaves coated with snow.

"She's heading to the river." Sheri caught up with Anna. She carried the bag with the bandana, which Anna must have dropped in her haste to follow the dog. "I brought this in case we needed it," Sheri said.

"Good idea," Anna said. If Jacquie lost the scent, they could use the bandana to refresh her memory. But for now, the dog was definitely keen. They reached the river and Jacquie waded right in, crashing through the ice on the shore into the rushing water. Anna moaned. If Jacquie decided to wade or swim across, she would need to follow, but she didn't relish doing so.

"That water isn't deep enough to drown in," Sheri said. "Did Dave decide to go fishing after all?"

But only a few steps into the water, Jacquie whirled around and headed south along the riverbank. Anna took a firmer grip on the long lead and stumbled after her, Sheri close behind. Jacquie veered around a large beaver dam and sniffed along the edge of the pond that had formed as a result of the beaver's efforts. She slowed, her nose pressed to the icy mud, snuffling loudly. The trainer Anna had worked with had explained that this snuffling was a way of pulling in more scent particles. Dogs had the ability to store up these particles. There was more ice here at this stiller water, and Anna studied it, searching for any sign that someone had fallen through. Dave liked to ice fish, but surely he would recognize this ice wasn't safe.

Jacquie tugged left, headed down a narrow path leading away from the pond. The neat imprints of deer hooves showed in the otherwise pristine snow of the trail. "She's not following the deer, is she?" Sheri asked.

Anna shook her head. Jacquie didn't do that. In the months since she had completed her training, she had proved to be an adept tracker, finding everything from lost hunters to—once—a discarded knife used in an assault along a jogging trail in Delta County.

Jacquie had slowed her pace, no longer eager, though her attention remained focused on the ground. Suddenly, she veered again, this time down another animal trail lined with wild roses, last year's hips crimson against clumps of snow. Jacquie barked and Anna looked up then pulled back on the leash. A wave of grief washed over her as she stared at the figure swaying from the tree branch in the midst of a grove of cottonwoods. She looked at the face only long enough to make sure it was Dave—contorted in death but recognizable by his neat goatee and hatchet nose.

Sheri pressed her palm to Anna's back. "I'm sorry," she whispered. "I was really, really hoping he had just gone fishing."

Anna turned her back to the body in the tree and called Jacquie. The dog came, tail down, head hanging. Though Anna told her she had done a good job and gave her treats and water, Jacquie knew finding a dead person was never as good as finding a live one. The dog had known Dave, too, and that probably made this even more upsetting for her.

"One of us needs to go back and get Deputy Malone and lead him back here," Sheri said. "I can stay here with the body while you do that."

"I'll wait here," Anna said.

Sheri frowned. "Are you sure?"

"It's all right." She looked up at the spreading

branches of a cottonwood, the thick gray bark patterned with orange and white lichen. "It's peaceful
here."

"Okay, then. It's liable to take a while. Will you
be okay?"

"I'll be okay." She offered a small smile. "I'm not
the hysterical type, and this isn't my first suicide recovery." The first had been a teenage boy who had
shot himself near the family's summer cabin. That
had been far worse, seeing those parents' grief. Staying here with Dave's body would be a last service
she could perform for him. And she would rather do
that than have to spend the long walk back in with
Lucas Malone, knowing what he must think of her
after that day in the hospital.

"All right," Sheri said. "I'll be back as soon as I
can." She turned and trotted away.

Anna led Jacquie back up the trail until she spotted a fallen log where she could sit. *Why had Dave
chosen to end his life here?* she wondered as she
contemplated the snow-covered scrub oaks and bare
trunks of cottonwoods. The county was full of more
scenic spots and places that were easier to get to.
Had he come here because he hadn't wanted to be
found? But parking his truck along the road guaranteed someone would eventually spot the vehicle and
make inquiries. People who didn't want to be found
at all tended to disappear in mountain wilderness,
miles from anyone, not within a quarter mile, as the
crow flies, from a road.

Jacquie leaned against Anna's thigh and rested

her head in Anna's lap. Anna combed her fingers through the dog's curly hair and thought about Dave. When was the last time she had seen him? Last Friday. She had gone into his shop to buy cookies to bring to a SAR meeting. He had smiled a big smile and clasped her hand warmly. "How are you doing?" he had asked, and looked into her eyes. "Tell me the truth."

"I'm good," she had said. "Things are starting to feel more…settled." She felt more in control of her life now, still missing Jonas, but the pain wasn't as intense. She could go whole days without thinking of her husband. She wasn't exactly happy, but she was content.

"I'm glad to hear it," he had said, and turned to box up her order, as usual throwing in a few extra cookies. The heady aromas of cinnamon, vanilla and chocolate perfumed the air of the shop, and she'd resisted the urge to tell him to add in one of the pink-frosted chocolate cupcakes in the display case. Surprise Cakes, the label read. That was one of Dave's specialties. The center of the cupcake was hollowed out and contained a surprise—a dollop of fruit filling or ganache, a marshmallow, nuts or a chocolate truffle. For Anna and Jonas's wedding, Dave had made a cupcake tower, each cupcake containing a silver charm.

I should have asked him how he was doing, she thought now. If she had, would he have told her the truth?

Jacquie's whimper interrupted her thoughts. The

dog was staring toward the clearing where Dave's body hung. "You don't want to go back there," Anna told her.

Jacquie stood and headed toward the clearing. "Jacquie, come back here," Anna called.

But the dog pretended not to hear. Anna caught up the end of the long lead before it slipped away and stood to follow.

At the clearing, Jacquie avoided the body but circled the area, sniffing among the trees. Anna shivered as a chill wind swept through, but she was grateful for the cold, which would keep down the smell. She told herself she shouldn't, but something in her compelled her to look again at the body.

Her first thought was that it was so high in the tree. Standing ten feet away, Dave's feet, in Merrell hiking boots with red laces and red trim, hung at about eye level. How in the world had he gotten up that high? More curious than horrified now—or maybe just numb—she walked to the base of the tree. It was an old cottonwood, with a trunk five feet thick or more, towering a hundred feet overhead. The trunk rose straight up ten feet before it divided. She didn't think she could have climbed it. But Dave had, and with a rope in his hand.

Jacquie had moved over to join her, then put her nose to the ground once more and headed toward the ground directly beneath the body. "Jacquie, come back," Anna called. She didn't think either one of them should be there. Maybe they were disturbing a crime scene. Well, not exactly a crime, but would the sheriff's department want to investigate?

Again, Jacquie played deaf. That wasn't really like her but, like people, dogs had moods, too, Anna had discovered. Maybe because she had been asked to find a dead person instead of a live one, today Jacquie was being contrary. The dog stopped now and alerted on something in the ground. With a growing sense of dread, Anna moved forward to see what had caught the dog's attention.

She stared at four square indentations in the ground beneath the body. They were deep enough to still be discernable in spite of the snow. The first two were about two feet apart. The second set was parallel to the first, three feet away. Anna stared. Where had she seen indentations like that before?

She thought to this summer when she had decided to repaint her bedroom. When she'd finished the job and cleaned up, she had found indentations just like those in the carpet, where the ladder she had used to reach the top of the wall had stood.

She looked around her, confused. If Dave had used a ladder to get into that tree, where was the ladder now?

Chapter Two

Lucas had been startled to run into Anna Trent in this remote setting. When the search and rescue captain had explained they were waiting for a canine search team, the name hadn't clicked for him. After all, it had been two years since he had last seen Anna, and a great deal had happened since then. But when he'd looked into her distressed blue eyes, he had been thrust back to that hospital corridor, in the glare of fluorescent lighting that made even healthy people look ill, listening to her rage against the inability— or as she'd seen it, unwillingness—of anyone to relieve her dying husband's pain.

The nurse Anna had been screaming at had welcomed Lucas's intervention. "Deputy, please take this woman away until she learns to control herself," she had said before stalking off.

Lucas hadn't responded out of any duty as a law enforcement officer. He had stopped by to see his girlfriend Jenny after a long shift, still in uniform, and had stepped into the corridor to allow a nurse to check a dressing and had heard the shouting and gone to see what was wrong. After the nurse left, Anna—he had only learned her name later, after checking at the nurses' station—turned on him. "If you're going to arrest anyone, it ought to be the people here for letting a man suffer so," she said and then burst into harsh, painful tears.

Lucas had held her until the front of his uniform shirt was soaked with her tears, and wanted to join right in with her. "I'm not going to arrest anyone," he said, though he doubted she heard him. If only dealing with life was as easy as locking up whoever was responsible for problems. Too often there was no one to blame and nothing to do but try to endure the pain.

They hadn't said anything else. When her tears had subsided a little, she jerked out of his arms, stared into his face with a horrified expression, and turned and ran down the corridor. He took a few steps after her, then decided maybe it was better if he left her. Sometimes suffering was easier done in private. At least, it was for him.

Now here they were, in another terrible situation. Anna looked better now. He had been aware of her beauty before, but in an abstract way. Today, her attractiveness was more concrete. He'd noticed the soft curve of her cheek and the deep blue of her eyes framed by dark lashes, and the lush pink of her lips. And he'd noticed that he'd noticed—something that hadn't happened to him in a long time.

Sheri jogged out of the underbrush and Lucas stepped from the SUV and went to meet her. "We found him," she said. "Hanging in a tree."

He grimaced. So the wife had been right to suspect suicide. "Anna is with him?" he asked.

"Someone had to stay and she insisted she could do it."

"Let me radio for the coroner and some more officers to help," he said. "Then you can show me."

The dispatcher promised to notify Dr. Butch Collins and to send two more officers to help retrieve the body. Then Lucas followed Sheri back into the underbrush. She set a brisk pace, moving more quickly than he would have thought for someone making the slog for the third time in the last hour. "I didn't like leaving Anna there alone," she said, as if to explain her haste. "I didn't want to leave her at all, but she insisted."

"You're sure it's suicide?" he asked.

Sheri stopped and looked back at him. "Are you saying someone else could have put him in that tree?"

"We can't assume anything," he said. "Every suspicious death has to be investigated."

She nodded. "But his wife said he was upset. She thought he might try to kill himself."

"I didn't see a note in the truck," Lucas said. "But we'll do a thorough search. And not everyone leaves a note." They set out walking again, not as fast now that the trail had narrowed and the going was more difficult. "Did you know him?"

"He ran the local bakery and he was a volunteer fireman," Sheri said. "I knew him to speak to, but not well." She paused. "You should ask Anna about him. Her late husband and Dave were good friends. Dave spoke at Jonas's funeral."

Hadn't the poor woman suffered enough? First, she'd lost her husband to cancer and now she had to find his friend's body? Lucas put his head down and trudged forward. A lot of things about his job were unpleasant, but today was moving to the top of his list of worst days on the force.

Anna met them on the trail before the clearing. She had a look about her Lucas had seen before. "What's wrong?" he asked.

"Maybe nothing." She pressed her lips together, as if uncertain whether she could continue. "I found something. Something that doesn't make sense."

"Show me." He started to follow her then turned to Sheri. "Stay here and wait for the others, please." No sense having anyone else in what could turn out to be a crime scene.

"I painted my bedroom recently," Anna said as she led the way up the trail. Most people would have wondered at the direction the conversation was taking, but Lucas had learned that many witnesses, especially witnesses under stress, preferred to approach explanations indirectly, sneaking up on a horrible truth. "When I was done, I noticed the ladder I'd used left impressions in the carpet." She glanced back at him. "There are impressions like that under Dave's body. But I can't find a ladder anywhere."

He put a hand out to stop her. "You saw these impressions in the snow?"

She nodded. "They're deep enough that the snow has settled into them. There was probably mud there before it snowed. We had a string of warm days before this latest storm."

"Did you see any footprints?" he asked. "Any disturbed ground?"

She shook her head. "No."

"Stay here," he said. "I'll go on and look for myself. How far is it to the body?"

"Not very far. You'll see a grove of cottonwoods. The body—Dave—is there."

He hurried past her and soon reached the cluster of cottonwoods. The man's body was near the center of the grove—a shocking, terrible sight. Lucas forced himself to study the image, to note the type of rope and position of the knot. Then he moved slowly toward the body, approaching at an oblique angle, studying the ground for any sign of footprints. He spotted fresh tracks in the heavier snow along the outer edge of the clearing from the woman and the dog, and partial shoe impressions moving toward the body. He thought these belonged to Anna.

He located the marks she had told him about and crouched down to study them. They definitely looked like indentations made by the legs of a ladder sunk deep into the mud, perhaps under the weight of a man. He glanced overhead again, trying to judge the height and weight of the body overhead. Not a small man, maybe as much as one-eighty to two hundred pounds. He stood and it struck him how high up the body was. If the ladder was, say, eight feet, and a six-foot-tall man stood on the step just below the top of the ladder, he could have just reached the branch the rope was tied to. So he fastened the rope and…then what? Jumped? Kicked over the ladder?

But where was the ladder?

He walked back to where Anna and the dog waited. "I see what you mean," he said. "We'll have to look into it."

"Does this mean Dave didn't kill himself?" she asked.

"We can't know at this point," Lucas said. "Sheri said you knew him?"

She nodded. "He and my husband were good friends."

"Sheri told me he died—your husband," he said. "I'm sorry for your loss."

She looked away. "Thank you."

He took a step backward. "You should go back to the parking area. I'll need to get a statement from you, but you can come into the sheriff's department this afternoon. I'll wait here for the coroner and the other deputies."

She nodded and gathered up Jacquie's leash.

"It was good seeing you again," he said. "Despite the circumstances."

She didn't say anything, merely looked at him a long moment then turned and walked down the trail. He waited until she was out of sight before he turned to walk back to the clearing and the ugly business of death.

ANNA AND JACQUIE emerged from the search area onto the road as two sheriff's department vehicles and a black SUV arrived. The vehicles parked behind Deputy Malone's SUV and half a dozen men emerged, including an older, portly man in a heavy overcoat, carrying a doctor's bag.

Sheriff Travis Walker, sporting a deep tan despite the winter weather, a souvenir of his recent tropical vacation, approached Anna and Jacquie. "Hello, Anna," he greeted her. "Lucas said you found the body pretty quickly."

"Jacquie took me right to him." She looked down at the dog, who raised her ears at the sound of her name.

"Not a fun job, I know, but you spared the family a longer wait."

"Deputy Malone said I need to give a statement," she said.

Travis seemed to consider this. "Let me talk to Lucas and someone will be in touch."

Then he left and she was alone, everyone else disappearing down the now-beaten trail through the snow. She walked over to Dave's truck. Careful not to touch anything, she looked into the cab. Funny, Dave had left the can of snuff behind—he usually kept it in his back pocket. All of his jeans had circles worn into the back pockets where the tins always nestled. But maybe he had emptied all his pockets before walking into the woods. Someone distressed enough to kill himself might have all kinds of ideas that didn't seem logical to her.

She turned away, back to her car, and drove the six miles to Eagle Mountain's main street. Traffic was light this time of year. The bulk of tourists would arrive with warmer weather, though several cars with out-of-state plates parked in front of the Cake Walk Café attested to ice climbers or skiers who appreciated the beauty of the mountains in winter. She turned into an alley and parked in a small lot behind the buildings that fronted Main.

Jacquie leaped out as soon as Anna opened the door and trotted to a green door at the rear of one of those buildings. Anna used her key to open the door and stepped into a narrow hallway flanked by a restroom on one side and a storage closet on the other. A buzzer announced her entrance and a round-faced woman with a tumble of shoulder-length gray curls looked down the hallway. "I wasn't expecting you in this morning," the woman said. "Are you okay?"

Gemma Taylor, Anna's sole employee and best friend, bent to pet Jacquie, who had scurried up to meet her, then straightened and regarded Anna. "From the look on your face, I'm guessing not well," she said.

"Not well." Anna hung her coat and Jacquie's leash on hooks beside the storeroom, then followed Gemma into the large front room of Yarn and More, the store she had opened last year.

Gemma moved a box of yarn from a chair at the long table at the back of the room. "Have a seat and I'll make some tea and you can tell me about it. Or not, if you'd rather not talk about it."

"I think I need to talk." Out in the field, she had been able to distance herself from what was happening, even after the shock of seeing Dave's body. Now the protective shell of adrenaline was dissolving, leaving her shaken. She needed to put things into words to process them. She sat and picked up a partially knitted scarf from a basket at the center of the table. She was working on a piece to use in a display of the New Mexico wool she had just begun to stock in the store.

Gemma slid a full mug toward Anna and sat across from her. "Your message said you were called on a search. Was it Dave?"

"It was Dave." She sipped the tea. It wasn't brewed enough yet, but the hot water soothed her anyway. "He's dead. Hanged."

Gemma gasped and put a hand to her mouth, then leaned across the table and gripped Anna's wrist. "I'm so sorry."

Anna nodded. "It's awful. And how horrible for Sandy. I'll have to call her later. After the sheriff's department has had time to notify her."

"Dave always seemed like such a happy guy," Gemma said. "But I guess you never know what's really going on with people."

Anna began to knit the scarf. The feel of the needles in her hand and the rhythm of the motion soothed her. Dave *was* a happy guy. In his early twenties, he had survived cancer and said he was grateful for every day he'd had since. Had his cancer returned? Or had something else happened to so drastically change his outlook?

But then there were those marks, as if from a

ladder. What did they mean? "I don't think I can talk about it anymore," she said. She wanted to tell Gemma about the ladder but maybe she should wait to see what the sheriff's department had to say about that. She nodded toward the box of yarn. That was a much safer topic of conversation right now. "I see that shipment of Malabrigo silky merino came in."

"Yes, and two cartons of hand-dyed sock yarn. The Sock Sisters will be pleased." The Sock Sisters were one of several knitting groups who met at the shop. Organizing such groups had been Gemma's idea, and a great strategy for recruiting regular customers.

"We've got four sign-ups for the spring break Knockout Knits class for teens," Gemma said. "I'm going to drop more flyers at the library and the Teen Explorers group. I'd love to have young people meeting here regularly. I want kids to know fiber arts aren't just for grandmas."

Anna smiled at her friend, who wore a deep red tunic sweater of her own design over patterned red leggings. "You don't look like anyone's grandma," she said.

Gemma grinned. "But speaking of grandmas— Jamie Douglas's neighbor came in first thing this morning with Jamie's sister, Donna. Turns out Donna has taken up knitting and they were looking for simple patterns she could make for the baby. I hooked her up with a couple of receiving blanket patterns, a soft knit cap to try, and some adorable but really simple diaper shirts and that baby yarn that's washable. I guess Jamie is on maternity leave for the next six weeks. The neighbor said the sheriff's department has an officer on loan from Mesa County while she's out."

"His name is Lucas Malone," Anna said.

"You've met him?" Gemma began removing hanks of yarn in a rainbow of colors from a box.

"He was the responding officer this morning. He opened Dave's truck so I could retrieve something for Jacquie to get Dave's scent."

Gemma leaned forward. "So, what's he like? How old is he? Is he single? Good-looking?"

"He's about thirty, I guess. Good-looking. Black hair, brown eyes. I have no idea whether he's married or not."

"Too young for me." Gemma went back to unboxing yarn. "But he's about your age."

"Don't get any ideas," Anna said, and cursed the blush that heated her cheeks.

"I was just making an observation." She picked up the empty box. "There are three more boxes of yarn to unpack, and we still have all the kits to put together for the Knockout Knits class."

The two women spent the rest of the morning into early afternoon unpacking new arrivals, adjusting displays and waiting on customers. Word of Dave Weiss's fate had apparently already spread and a couple of the women who'd stopped in had clearly hoped to glean more information. A terse "I really don't want to talk about it" from Anna had sent them on their way.

A little after four, the chime on the door signaled a new arrival. Anna emerged from the back room to find Deputy Malone standing before a large display of variegated sock yarn. "Are you a knitter, Deputy?" she asked.

He took a step away from the yarn. "No, um, I came to see you."

Jacquie trotted over to greet him and he bent to scratch her head. "Is something wrong?" Anna asked. Her heart pounded.

"I need to get your statement and thought it might be easier for me to come to you." He straightened and looked around the shop, his gaze pausing briefly at the table, where two women had stopped knitting to stare at him. "If there's somewhere we can talk?"

"I'll watch things up here while you and the deputy use the back office," Gemma said.

Anna widened her eyes at Gemma. The back office was what Gemma insisted on calling the storeroom whenever there was someone around she wanted to impress. But it wasn't a real office, and it was scarcely large enough for two people.

"That would be great," Malone said. He and Gemma both turned to her and the awkward moment stretched.

"Fine," she said at last. "Come this way, Deputy." She swiveled on her heel and led the way to the storeroom. At least if she embarrassed herself any more in front of the deputy, she could do it surrounded by yarn she loved.

Chapter Three

The room—more of a large closet—Anna led Lucas to held one of those high-top tables he had seen in bars, the surface all of two feet square, with two spindly-looking metal chairs. The rest of the room was filled with yarn—yarn of every color spilling from shelves, some in boxes or baskets or bags, other balls of it loose in pyramids and piles. A wooden crate on the floor held still more yarn and a box next to it was filled with packages of knitting needles.

"This isn't really an office," Anna said, as if reading his puzzlement. "It's our store room. But it's the only private place in the shop unless you want to try to squeeze into the bathroom."

"This will do." He pulled out one of the chairs. "Let's sit down."

She perched on the edge of her seat and he settled into the chair across from her, which squeaked under his weight. Their knees brushed before she angled hers away. He pretended not to notice, though the zing of awareness lingered. "How long have you had this place?" he asked, making conversation, trying to put her at ease as he pulled out his digital recorder and a statement form.

"A little over a year." She looked around at the rainbow of yarns. "I had some insurance money from Jonas, and this building came open. There isn't a good fiber store within a hundred miles of Eagle Mountain, so I thought I'd take a chance."

He nodded. "I'm going to be recording this," he said. "Could you go ahead and state your name for the recording."

"Oh. Sure. Anna Simmons Trent."

"And you were at the scene this morning in what capacity?"

"I was there with my search dog, Jacquie. I'm a volunteer with Eagle Mountain Search and Rescue and we had been asked to help look for a missing person, Dave Weiss."

"Tell me about your search and what you found. Start at the beginning."

She took a deep breath and paused, as if gathering her thoughts. "I met Sheri Stevens at Search and Rescue headquarters at seven thirty and followed her to the location where Dave's truck had been found." Then she took him through the rest of the morning, up to the moment she had located Dave Weiss's body hanging in a cottonwood tree.

"Describe the scene for me, please," he said.

"It was—remote," she said. "But not really. As the crow flies, it's only about a quarter mile from the Forest Service road. The map we consulted labeled the area Panther Point, but there aren't any named hiking trails around there. And the trail we followed in wasn't made by hikers or hunters or anything like that. It was an animal trail. I don't think it's a place anyone would go to fish or even to take pictures."

"Do you think that's significant?" he asked.

"How did Dave even know about it? Why would he have been there at all? He went to a lot of trouble to get back there, but why there?"

"Do you have any idea?"

"None."

"What else did you notice while you were waiting for Sheri to return with law enforcement?"

"Jacquie was restless. She insisted on sniffing around under the body. I thought she was upset because it was Dave and she knows him. Sometimes when I stop by his bakery, he gives her a treat. He *gave* her a treat." She looked down for a moment, gathering herself.

"Would you like me to get you some water?" he asked.

"No. I'm okay." She took a deep breath. "I followed her, trying to get her to come away from the area, but she stopped right beneath the body, sniffing at something on the ground. That's when I saw the impressions of what looked like a ladder."

"The impressions were on top of the snow?"

"No, it had snowed on top of them, filling them in partially, but not all the way."

"What made you think a ladder made those marks?"

"I remembered when I painted my bedroom, the ladder left impressions just like that in the carpet."

"Did you notice anything else?"

She hesitated.

"Anything at all could be useful," he said.

"The body was up really high. Like—ten feet in the air. That seemed really high up for someone to be hanging if they did it themselves. And the tree he was in was really big, and it was a long way up before there were any good branches to climb. Dave was a volunteer fireman and he was in good shape, but I wondered how he got up that tree."

"Did you notice how the rope was tied?"

She shook her head. "No. Why?"

"I'm just wanting your impressions." The rope had been secured fairly low around the trunk of the tree. Accessible to someone standing on the ground but, to his mind, awkward for that same person to then drape the other end over that high branch. Not impossible, though.

"Has anyone told Sandy?" Anna asked. "Dave's wife?"

"Yes. The sheriff and I notified her that her husband's body had been found."

"Poor woman. I'll have to go see her. She must be devastated."

"She was obviously very upset." She had stared at Lucas and the sheriff for a long moment then burst into noisy sobs. Lucas had summoned a neighbor to sit with her, but Sandy had been too grief-stricken to answer any of their questions. He would need to talk to her soon, though.

"Do you really think Dave killed himself?" Anna

asked. "I know Sandy told the dispatcher he was worried about financial problems, but was he really that upset? Was there anything else?"

"Mrs. Weiss wasn't able to speak with us," he said. "But, apparently, when she reported her husband as missing, she'd said he had taken out loans to expand his business and was having trouble meeting the payments."

"I didn't know he was expanding his business."

"I understand he was friends with your late husband."

"Yes. And my friend, too, after Jonas and I married. He was a big help after Jonas died. But I hadn't seen much of him in the last six months."

"Why is that?"

She shrugged. "I think maybe Sandy might have been jealous of the attention he was giving me. There was never a hint of anything untoward between us, but I got the impression, from little things he said, that she was the jealous type. But I was doing better on my own, and Dave had plenty to do between looking after his business and his volunteer work. I still saw him when I shopped at the bakery and he never acted any differently toward me."

"Had you seen him recently?"

"I saw him Friday. He seemed fine."

"What about Mrs. Weiss? How well do you know her?"

"Not as well. Jonas and I spent a lot of time with her and Dave—barbecues at their house, dinners at ours, things like that. The guys were best friends and they wanted us to be friends, too. Sandy and I get along fine, but we're so different. She never said anything, but I got the impression she didn't approve of me. Or she thought I wasn't good enough for Jonas."

"What about her marriage? Did she and her husband get along?"

Anna stared at him. "You can't think Sandy had anything to do with Dave's death. The two of them adored each other. And they did everything together. They ran the bakery together and they were both firefighters. When they were younger, they competed in body-building competitions. That's how they met. They were really a team."

"It's just a routine question."

"Does this mean you don't think Dave took his own life? Someone with a ladder? Someone who could have put the rope that high?"

"It's much too early to draw any conclusions," he said. "Is there anything else you noticed that might be significant or that seemed unusual to you?"

"Dave left his tin of snuff in his truck," she said. "That was odd because he always carried it in his back pocket." She frowned. "I don't see how that could be significant, it just struck me as odd."

"Anything else?"

"No. I just…is it okay if I contact Sandy? We weren't close, but I want to offer my condolences and any help she might need."

"Of course. I told her you were the one to find the body."

"She would have figured that out soon enough.

Anyway, I want to talk to her. I probably come closer than most to know how she's feeling right now, widowed so young."

"Is there anything else that struck you as unusual or significant about the place where you and your search dog located the body?" he asked.

She shook her head. "No."

He leaned over and switched off the recorder. "When did your husband die?" he asked. "If you don't mind my asking."

"I don't mind. It happened not long after that day in the hospital." She didn't say what day—she didn't have to. "He slipped into a coma and never woke up."

"I'm sorry," he said again. She was younger than Sandy Weiss. Under thirty. She couldn't have been married that long.

"I shouldn't have yelled at that nurse the way I did," she said. "It wasn't her fault. It wasn't anyone's fault. But I couldn't let him suffer that way and do nothing."

"It's okay," he said. "No one is blaming you. Least of all me."

"I apologized to her after Jonas died. It was…awkward." She covered her face with one hand. "I had this idea when Jonas was first diagnosed that I was going to be so patient and loving and gracious. I wasn't anything like that. It was…so ugly."

"Yeah. It's like that."

She lowered her hand and her eyes met his, clear and laser-focused. "You know?"

He concentrated on putting away the recorder and

his notepad. "I wasn't at the hospital that night because someone had called me about you," he said. "I was there because my girlfriend was there. She died, too. Three months after your husband."

Her face crumpled a little, eyes crinkled, mouth compressed, expression turned more inward. "I'm sorry."

"I used to get pretty frustrated with things at the hospital, too," he said. "The person in that bed is your whole focus and to the staff they're just one more needy person they are trying to care for. Not that they were callous, but everyone can't be their priority the way your loved one is for you."

"I wish I had been more understanding, that's all," she said. "But I do feel better knowing the hospital didn't call you in to arrest me." She stood and he rose, also. He looked at her across that tiny table and became aware once more of how intimate this space was. There was scarcely room for one of them to move without touching the other.

"I think someone who gives up her time to go out and search for other people, in rough terrain and all kinds of weather, has a lot of compassion," he said. "That's more important than one outburst at a weak moment."

"Thank you for saying that. I hope you find out what really happened to Dave. And why."

"The whys are a lot harder to figure out sometimes."

"I guess so."

She started to move past him to open the door

and jostled against him. They both jumped away, as if shocked, and she laughed nervously. "Maybe we should have met at the sheriff's department."

"No, this was better," he said. He liked being close to her. He hadn't felt that way about a woman since Jenny had died. He took it as a good sign.

ANNA PHONED SANDY that evening after she got home, but no one answered her call. She hung up without leaving a message. She couldn't say anything to make the situation better, but at least she could offer her sympathy in person, where she was sure it would mean more than a recorded message.

She moved into the kitchen to feed Jacquie and her gaze came to rest on a framed photo on the refrigerator—she and Jonas, Dave and Sandy, all standing atop Dakota Ridge the summer before Jonas became ill. The men stood together in the middle—both tall, fit and handsome, flanked by the women. Sandy was only a few inches taller than Anna's five feet, three inches, but stockier and more muscular. She had very short blond hair and light blue eyes, and looked directly at the camera, grinning widely to show the slight gap between her upper front teeth. Anna was looking at Jonas, leaning into his side. Pain pinched at her heart, remembering that day. She had thought their whole long future together stretched out ahead of them.

Jacquie whined, reminding her what she was supposed to be doing. She measured out the dog's food and set it on the floor, and wondered what Sandy was doing right now. The evening after Jonas had died, Anna had wandered through this house feeling detached from reality. Jacquie had been only a year old, just starting her search and rescue training, and looking after her had been Anna's only tether to routine. Jacquie had had to be fed and walked and petted and played with. She'd had to practice her search techniques several times a week and attend classes and training. Having her to focus on had helped Anna so much.

Sandy and Dave hadn't had a dog or any children, so what was Sandy focusing on?

Anna regretted telling Deputy Malone that Sandy hadn't liked her. They had never been close, but Sandy had never been rude or said anything negative to Anna. They were just very different people. Anna liked reading, knitting, and growing flowers. Sandy raced dirt bikes, fished, and hunted. She was competent and competitive, and Anna had felt awkward around her. Anna had even worried that she was the kind of woman Jonas admired and secretly preferred, though those fears had gradually left her.

When Jonas had died, Sandy and Dave had brought a tray of pastries and offered to drive Anna to the funeral. Sandy had wept alongside Anna and kept people away when the condolence calls became too much for Anna. Anna wanted to do the same for her.

Tomorrow, she told herself as she shut off the light for the night. Tomorrow she would go to Sandy and do what she could to help.

SHORTLY BEFORE TEN the next morning, Anna headed to Yarn and More to open the store. Gemma had Wednesday mornings off and, if the store was quiet during that time, Anna would catch up on some bookwork. But she was surprised to find Sandy waiting at the back entrance to the store. She had the hood of her blue parka pulled up, shielding her face from view, but there was no mistaking her sturdy frame.

"Could I talk to you for a minute?" Sandy asked as Anna exited her car, before Anna could even say hello.

"Of course. Come in." She hurried to unlock the back door and ushered Sandy inside. Jacquie followed, her attention focused on their visitor.

"Sit down and let me take your coat," Anna said, gesturing to the wooden worktable. "I'll make us some coffee. Or would you rather have tea?"

"Nothing." Sandy sat but didn't remove her parka. "I just want to ask you a few questions then get out of here before anyone sees me."

"Of course." Anna pulled a chair out to face Sandy. She would leave the Closed sign in place a little longer. A large shelf of yarn would hide them from the view of anyone peering in the front windows. "I'm so sorry about Dave," she said. "This must have come as a huge shock."

"Everyone's sorry," Sandy said. "I'm sick of hearing about it. All the sorry in the world isn't going to bring him back."

Anna started to say how sorry she was about that,

but stopped herself in time. "What do you need from me?" she asked. "I'll do anything I can to help."

"The sheriff and that other cop who came to see me yesterday said you were the one who found Dave's body."

"Yes. Jacquie and I were called in to search." Jacquie moved to rest her head in Anna's lap and Anna fondled her soft ears.

"They said his truck was parked on a forest road, down near the river. That kind of marshy spot past Panther Point."

"Yes."

"Where exactly? The cops didn't give me a lot of details."

"The truck was parked on the side of the road, nosed up in some oak brush," Anna said. "Jacquie and I followed a game trail to the river, then down to where a beaver dam had formed a pond, then past that to a grove of cottonwoods. Dave was in the cottonwoods."

"Hanging. They said he hanged himself."

Even though she had been there and seen it for herself, the words sounded so harsh and ugly to Anna. But then, the situation was harsh and ugly. "Yes," she said.

Sandy nodded and said nothing else. She had dark circles under her eyes and looked drained but still strong. She wasn't the type of woman to ever look fragile, Anna supposed. She had often envied Sandy's physical prowess, but she saw now that her strength went deeper.

"Why would Dave go there?" Anna asked. "Do you know?"

"No idea." Sandy shook her head. "There aren't any good ski trails back in there, and it's too close to the road for legal hunting. And it's too marshy for fishing."

"So you know the area?" Anna asked.

Sandy's eyes met hers and there was no mistaking the disdain in her expression. "I've lived in this county all my life. There isn't any place I don't know."

"Of course." She stared down at her lap, once again feeling awkward. It annoyed her. No one else she knew made her feel this way.

"You said something about this being a shock," Sandy said. "Well, it was and it wasn't. I knew Dave was stressed out, but I never thought he'd take the coward's way out like this."

Anna felt the anger behind the words. That was part of grief, she remembered—being so angry at the person who had left. "Why was he stressed out?" she asked.

She half expected Sandy to tell her that was none of her business, but instead she said, "About six months ago, we were approached by this restaurant supplier who offered us a way to expand the business. This guy agreed to buy desserts from us. He'd distribute them to restaurants in the area. Locally sourced food is a big selling point these days, and Dave had built up a reputation for his pies and especially those Surprise Cakes. It was too good a deal to pass up—too good to be true, really." Sandy pressed her lips together and the fine lines around her eyes tightened.

"If it was such a good deal, why was Dave stressed?" Anna asked.

"We had to take out a loan to add another walk-in cooler, to hire another baker, and purchase more cookie sheets and muffin tins and another commercial-grade mixer. It was a big investment, but we were sure it would pay off. But the money coming in wasn't as much as this guy had promised, and the commissions we owed him for every sale took a big chunk of our profits, so we were really squeezed."

"What's going to happen now?" Anna asked.

"I'm trying to get out of having to pay off the loans," Sandy said. She seemed calm enough. "That may mean losing the business. We never should have agreed to the deal in the first place, but Dave was really excited about it, at least at first."

"But would he really have killed himself over something like this?" Anna asked.

"He did, didn't he?" Sandy glared at her.

"What if he didn't?" Anna asked.

In the silence that followed, Anna could hear Sandy breathing. Jacquie whimpered then lay down, her chin resting on Anna's shoe.

"What do you mean?" Sandy finally asked. "Dave hung himself. The sheriff said so."

"Did he say it like that, exactly?" Anna asked.

Sandy frowned. "He said they found Dave's body hanging in a cottonwood tree near the river. His truck was parked nearby. There wasn't anybody else there."

She leaned toward Anna. "That's right, isn't it? You didn't see anyone else there, did you?"

"No. But it was just such a strange place for him to go to die. His body was so high up in that tree. How did he ever climb it?"

"Dave was a good climber. He would scramble up any trail. He did rock climbing, and he could shimmy right up a tree. I've seen him do it."

"Maybe so." She hesitated. Should she say anything about the marks she had seen on the ground? She couldn't be sure if they were made by a ladder. But if she were in Sandy's place, she would want to know. "There were some marks on the ground underneath the body," she began.

"What kind of marks?" Sandy demanded, her voice sharp.

"Some indentations, like from the legs of a ladder."

Sandy let out a bark of not-quite laughter. "Are you saying somebody hauled a ladder out there and strung up Dave's body? You do know the man weighed over a hundred and eighty pounds? And you probably haven't carried around too many ladders in your life, but let me tell you, they're heavy and they're awkward. It's not something you want to lug around in a bunch of underbrush, through frozen swamp. If someone did want to kill Dave, there were a lot easier ways to do it."

Anna could see how absurd the situation was when Sandy described it like that. But was it any more absurd than a man taking his own life? "I'm just telling you what I saw. The sheriff's department is investigating and I'm sure they'll come to the right conclusion."

"The only conclusion is that Dave killed himself." Sandy knotted her hands in her lap. "I know he looked happy and upbeat to everyone, but take it from me, he had his dark moods. And he grew up without a lot of money. He had a real fear of being poor. He thought we'd default on our loan and lose the business and be out in the street. I tried to tell him he was being foolish, talking like that, but he wouldn't listen to me."

"You certainly know him better than anyone," Anna said.

"I wondered why the sheriff asked me if Dave had any enemies. I guess I know now. But everybody liked Dave. The customers liked him. The other firefighters liked him. They liked him more than they like me."

"You have a lot of friends in this town, Sandy," Anna said. "I know it can be hard to accept help from others, but if you need it, don't hesitate to ask. You're going to have a lot to deal with now that Dave is gone."

"I'll handle it." She stood. "Most people don't know this, but I'm the one who's kept the business going for years. Dave was good at baking, but he was really lousy with money. He worried about making those loan payments, but I knew we'd be all right. Part of being successful in business is knowing when to cut your losses and move on. That's what I'm going to do now."

Anna rose, also. "If there's anything I can do to help, please let me know," she said. "You and Dave were such a help to me after Jonas died."

"Like you said, I've got plenty of friends who will help me if I need it." She nodded. "I can let myself out. You'd better open up before some woman with a yarn emergency gets upset."

Anna watched until Sandy had let herself out the back door then went to the front door, unlocked it and turned the sign to Open. Was that "yarn emergency" remark Sandy's attempt at humor or a way to belittle her and her customers? And what should she make of that comment about Sandy having friends who could help her? It was only as much as Anna herself had said.

Still, the words stung. Sandy had always had a way of getting under her skin.

One of the Sock Sisters came in to look at the new shipment of sock yarn, and another regular wanted help figuring out the directions in a pattern for a sweater she was knitting. Anna made a few other sales, paid some invoices, filed others, and finished up a new display of crochet thread. At twelve thirty, she had just finished eating the sandwich she had brought from home when Kyle Saddler came in.

"Hey, Anna," he said, offering a shy smile.

A tall man who hunched his shoulders as if to appear smaller, Kyle was another friend of Jonas's who had, by default, become Anna's friend, too. As the county building inspector, he'd frequently gone to Jonas's job sites to approve the work Jonas had completed. Lately, he had also made a habit of stopping by Yarn and More.

"What can I help you with today, Kyle?" Anna asked.

He looked around, as if suddenly remembering where he was. "Um, my niece is turning ten next week," he said. "She likes crafty stuff, so I thought maybe…some yarn?" The shy smile again. "Could you help me pick out something she would like?"

"Sure." She led the way to the display of needles and notions on the side wall. "We have some Learn to Knit kits geared toward teens and tweens that I bet she would enjoy." She pulled one of the kits from the hook. "This comes with yarn, instructions, needles and a link to a video she can watch to help with the basics."

Kyle took the kit. "Great. I'll take it."

She was walking toward the cash register when Gemma rushed in from the back. She stopped short when she saw Kyle. "I forgot something in my car," she stammered, whirled around, and exited again.

"Is there anything else?" Anna asked as she rang up Kyle's purchase.

"Yeah," he said.

She looked up at his emphatic tone and met his steady gaze. "Would you have dinner with me this weekend?" he asked.

Her stomach dropped to her toes. Kyle looked so hopeful. And he was so nice. "That's so sweet of you to ask," she said. "But I'm not really interested in dating again. Not yet."

"I understand." He handed her his credit card. "I was just thinking, though. It's been two years. You're still a young woman. Maybe you should try going out. With a friend."

She processed the card then handed it back to him. "I'm just not ready," she said.

His smile was gone, replaced by a woeful look. He tucked his wallet into his back pocket. "Let me know if you change your mind."

The door hadn't fully closed behind him before Gemma hurried in from the back room. "Didn't I tell you?" she said, equal parts censure and triumph in her voice. "Kyle Saddler didn't take a sudden interest in yarn because he wanted a new hobby. He wanted you!"

Anna tucked the credit card slip into the cash register drawer and pushed it shut. "Kyle is a very nice man, but I'm not interested in dating anyone."

"Why not?" Gemma asked. Her expression softened. "I'm not saying you have to get involved with anyone, but dinner wouldn't hurt."

"Kyle wants a lot more than dinner." At thirty-four, Kyle had said more than once that he was ready to settle down. When she looked in his eyes, she saw "serious romance" not "casual friendship."

"You're too young to spend the rest of your life alone," Gemma said. She patted Anna's hand. "I'm only saying that because I love you."

"I know," Anna said. "I'm just...not ready." Though, lately, something inside her had shifted. If the right man—someone she was attracted to, who wouldn't expect too much—came along, she might at least agree to go out. Maybe. The thought made her stomach twist in knots, but life was all about taking risks, right?

"I stopped by Sandy Weiss's house on the way over here," Gemma said as she moved to the work-table. She had shed her coat to reveal a colorwork sweater in shades of purple and green. "She wasn't there, but did you know there's a For Sale sign in the yard?"

"No. I spoke to Sandy this morning and she never said anything about that."

"You went by the house and the sign wasn't there?"

"No. She was waiting for me at the back door when I got to work this morning."

"Then she probably didn't tell you the bakery is for sale, too. There's no sign there, but I called the real estate agent who has the listing for the house and pretended to be interested and she said the business is for sale, too."

"Gemma, you didn't!"

"I'm sure I'm not the only one." Gemma set a large pink travel mug on the end of the worktable. "Barely twenty-four hours since Dave's body was found and Sandy has already contacted a broker?"

"That does seem really sudden," Anna said. "But Sandy mentioned something about money problems. Maybe she feels like she needs to sell out to pay debts Dave left."

"You would think she would at least wait a week or two," Gemma said. "Don't they tell people dealing with grief not to make any drastic, life-changing decisions too quickly?"

"Yes." But when your life had already been changed so completely by the death of a person you loved, everything else seemed secondary. In the days following Jonas's death, Anna had considered selling the house and moving away, even though she and Jonas had talked about her staying. At least she had had time to discuss those things with him before he died. Sandy hadn't had that luxury. "I'm sure she's doing what she thinks she needs to do," she said. "This has got to be really hard for her."

"I'm sure it is, but selling out? Where is she going to go? She's lived here all her life."

"Her parents died several years ago," Anna said. "And her siblings moved away. Maybe she thinks now that Dave is gone, there's nothing here for her. Maybe she wants to make a fresh start. She said she was ready to cut her losses and move on."

"She's certainly not wasting any time," Gemma said. "People are going to talk. They're going to wonder what she's running away from."

Maybe she was running from grief, Anna thought. Plenty of people had tried, though they all learned, as she had, that unlike justice or retribution, grief always caught up with you.

Chapter Four

"He died from a broken neck." Rayford County Medical Examiner Dr. Butch Collins looked down on the body of Dave Weiss, arranged on a metal table in the basement room that served as his lab and the county morgue. A stocky man with the weathered face of someone who spent a lot of time outdoors, he had the calm, matter-of-fact delivery of someone who had seen it all and was surprised by nothing. "Nothing unexpected about that. From what I saw at the scene, that tree branch he was tied to was high enough off the ground to ensure a big drop."

"So that's how he did it—climbed up there, put the noose around his neck and jumped?" Lucas asked.

"That would have done it," Collins said.

"We didn't see any marks on the tree trunk or limb to show he had climbed up there," Travis said. The sheriff and Lucas had driven to the medical examiner's office shortly after 11:00 a.m. on Wednesday, after two hours going over the scene at Panther Point again. "I don't think I could have made that climb."

"Dave was pretty athletic," Collins said. "Maybe he had practiced and knew he could get up there."

"Anything else?" Travis asked.

"He had a hefty dose of barbiturates in his system. Looks like he washed them down with a strawberry-banana smoothie. Phenobarbital."

"Where would he get his hands on phenobarbital?" Lucas asked.

"We don't prescribe it much for people these days," Collins said. "But it's fairly common in veterinary medicine. They use it to treat seizures in dogs."

"Dave didn't have a dog," Travis said.

"Then maybe he knew someone who did? Or he got a doctor to prescribe it for him?" Collins shrugged. "I can't help you there. In any case, the pills didn't kill him—the fall did."

"So why take them?" Lucas asked.

"He took enough to calm him down some. Maybe to give him the courage to go through with it."

"So he climbed that tree while he was doped up?" Travis asked.

"Adrenaline can negate the effect of sedatives to a certain extent," Collins said.

"Could someone have doped him up, hauled him out to that tree and strung him up?" Lucas asked.

"If you're skeptical Dave climbed that tree by himself, what makes you think someone else could climb up there with him?" Collins asked.

"What if they had a ladder?" Travis asked. "Force him to climb up the ladder, maybe at gunpoint, put the noose around his neck, then shove him off, or kick the ladder away."

"They'd have to have a lot of physical strength. Dave wasn't a little guy, and even drugged, he would probably fight back."

"But would the injuries you saw be consistent with that scenario?" Travis asked.

"They would." Collins regarded Dave's still features. "He's got some bruising on his arms and legs, but he was an active guy and they're the kind of marks anyone who's into rock climbing, skiing, hauling around big bags of flour and fire hoses and whatever else might have on them. Nothing unusual under his fingernails, no signs that he fought anyone." He looked back up at them. "That's it. I didn't find anything that isn't consistent with suicide."

"Thanks, Butch." Travis nodded and they turned to go.

Back in the sheriff's SUV, Travis started the engine but didn't move out of the parking spot. "What do you think?" he asked.

"I think suicides are usually suicides," Lucas said.

"And why would anyone kill Dave Weiss?" Travis said. "His wife says he was distressed. He's athletic enough to have climbed that tree himself."

"What about the ladder marks? That's the only sticking point for me."

"We don't know they were from a ladder," Travis said. "Maybe they were from rocks someone dug up? Or impressions made weeks ago." He shook his head. "The easiest explanation is usually the right one."

"So Dave Weiss killed himself?"

"Unless we find other evidence to the contrary, yes. Did Anna Trent's statement turn up anything of interest?"

Other than the fact that I'm attracted to her? "No, sir," Lucas said. "She noted the same things we did, about the height of the rope and the indentations in the mud and snow. Oh, and she thought it was odd that Dave left his snuff in the vehicle."

"People who are distraught can vary from their usual routines," Travis said. "I can't see any significance in snuff in the truck and not in his pocket."

Lucas shifted. "I'd still like to interview the widow," he said. "I want to hear what she thinks now that she's hopefully not as distraught as she was yesterday."

"Talk to her. Then give me a final report and we'll close this out."

"Yes, sir." The sheriff was right, yet those indentations in the mud and snow still bothered him. He didn't like unanswered questions and loose ends, but only on television did a case end with all of those tied in neat bows.

ALL DAY WEDNESDAY, Anna kept returning to her conversation with Sandy. Why had this mysterious businessman approached Dave—owner of a small bakery in a small town—to make a deal to supply desserts for restaurants? Yes, Dave was an excellent baker, but was his reputation that widespread? Was the man buying from many small bakeries or only from Dave? And why would Dave, who had always said he was content with the life he had, suddenly decide to take on the stress of expanding his business? He and Sandy didn't have children to provide for, and Dave had sometimes joked about how he was "the opposite of ambitious."

After she returned home that evening, she called the one person she thought might help her understand the situation better. Justin Trent, Jonas's older brother, answered her call on the second ring. "Anna! What are you doing calling me?" he said, raising his voice to be heard over the clink of glasses and hum of conversation. She pictured him, a stouter, grayer version of Jonas, with swept-back salt-and-pepper hair and a runner's lean frame, standing in the bar of Red Mesa, the restaurant he owned in downtown Junction.

"I was talking with a friend today and heard something that piqued my interest," she said. "I thought you might be able to give me some more information."

"Information about what?" The background noise ended abruptly. He must have moved to his office, behind the bar.

"Do you remember Dave Weiss?" she asked. "Jonas's good friend?"

"The baker, right? I think I met him a time or two."

"He was found dead yesterday. It may have been suicide."

"That's terrible. I'm sorry, Anna. And his wife is a friend of yours?"

"Yes." No point explaining all the background or

that she was the one who'd found the body. "She said Dave was really stressed because he had taken out loans to expand his bakery business and was having trouble repaying them."

"It happens," Justin said. "People get in over their heads. What does this have to do with me? No offense, but I've got a full house tonight and I really need to get back out there."

"I won't keep you long," she said. "Dave's wife said a man approached him six months ago and offered to buy all the desserts he could provide, at a very good price, to supply area restaurants who want to advertise that they use local products. Do you know anything about that?"

"She's probably talking about George Anton," he said. "We use his company for some of the items we serve at Red Mesa. He's negotiated some really competitive prices for local meat, vegetables and baked goods. The suppliers get a good profit, restaurant owners like me get to offer a quality, local product to customers at a price point where I can still make money."

"So it's legitimate?"

"Why would you think it wouldn't be?" Momentary static as he moved around. "What's really going on, Anna? What do you care about this other guy's business dealings?"

"Jacquie and I found his body," she said. "We were called to help after Dave was reported missing and his truck was found, abandoned. I was there at the scene and I'm just not sure it was suicide. Dave had no reason to kill himself."

"Whoa, there. What do the local police say? What does the man's widow say?"

"His wife—his widow—thinks he killed himself. I don't know that the sheriff's department has decided."

"You need to stay out of this and let them do their job. It isn't any business of yours. I'm sorry about your friend but, seriously, don't think you can play amateur detective. Real life isn't like TV."

"I'm aware of that, Justin." She clenched her jaw. How could she have forgotten Justin's insufferable superior attitude? He had always—but especially since Jonas had died—treated Anna as if she didn't have the brains to find her way across town. When he'd learned she'd planned to open Yarn and More, he had accused her of throwing away Jonas's life insurance money. He told her to sell the house, move to the city, and go back to school to get a degree in something that would allow her to support herself.

"Maybe you need to find some volunteer activities to devote yourself to," he said. "That little yarn store you opened obviously isn't keeping you busy enough. Or I can always use help at the restaurant. We could probably set you up in a little apartment here in Junction, where I'd be close enough to help you when you need a hand. Jonas would have liked that, I think."

Jonas would have hated that, she was sure. And if she ever needed a job, Justin would be the last person she would ask to hire her. "Thank you for answering my question," she said. "How is Gloria?"

His pause was too long—he was probably framing how to word his answer. "Gloria is good," he said finally. "She and I are good together. I made a mistake and she's forgiven me."

"That's good to hear," Anna said, though she wasn't so sure. She liked her sister-in-law, and she had seen how hurt Gloria had been when she'd discovered Justin's affair with a coworker. Jonas had been furious with his brother, but Justin had dismissed his concern. "I know how to handle myself," he had said. But, apparently, he had done the right thing and gotten back together with his wife. "I'm happy for you," she said.

"Whether you are or you aren't doesn't really matter to me. I have to go now."

Silence, indicating he had ended the call. She stared at the screen, then stowed her phone once more. Talking with Justin always left her irritated, but at least he had satisfied her curiosity about Dave's new business venture. Apparently, it was legit, and she had a name, too. George Anton. Nothing she had learned contradicted what Sandy had told her. Dave had made a business deal that hadn't worked out the way he'd hoped, he had gotten in a financial bind and been so upset at the results he couldn't live with himself. It was upsetting and, in many ways, unfathomable, but that didn't make it any less true. Maybe this was the case in all suicides—they never made sense to the grieving people left behind.

A text pulled her from her reverie and she read the summons from Search and Rescue.

Lost hiker. Sunshine Ridge trail.

Before she could respond that she was on her way, a second text arrived. This one from Sheri.

I think we need you and Jacquie on this.

We're on our way, Anna typed then went to retrieve Jacquie's harness and her pack.

DIANE SEYMORE, described as a fit, fifty-seven-year-old woman who hiked every week year-round, had failed to return to her condo after telling her neighbor she was going to hike Sunshine Ridge if the trail was clear enough of ice. Lucas had driven to the trailhead and found Diane's vehicle, but no sign of the missing hiker, and summoned Search and Rescue.

"I walked about half a mile down the trail before a snowslide blocked the path," he told the Search and Rescue volunteers who met him at the trail, including, he couldn't help but notice, Anna Trent and her dog, Jacquie. "I could see what looked like fairly fresh prints from a smaller-sized hiking boot until that point. I called out for Diane Seymore, but didn't get an answer."

"It's possible she was caught in the snowslide," one of the volunteers, a tall, thin man the others addressed as Tony, said.

"Or she might have tried to go around the slide," Carrie Andrews said.

"We could waste valuable time trying to figure out the best place to look," Captain Sheri Stevens said. She studied the sky. "The sun is going to set behind that ridge in less than an hour. We need to get Anna and Jacquie on this before the trail goes any colder."

"I'll open Diane's car so you can retrieve a scent article," Lucas said. He'd been thinking a lot about Anna since they had last talked. Being near her made him feel more alive and awake than he had in the two years since Jenny had died from cancer. Those were feelings he wanted to hold on to after being numb for so long.

She followed him from his department SUV to Diane's Jeep. Jacquie pranced on the end of her leash ahead of them. She had the traditional poodle cut, with pom-poms of curly hair around her wrists and ankles, another pom-pom on the end of her stubby tail. But her orange Search Dog vest and intense focus marked her as a working animal, ready to get down to business.

Anna trotted along behind the eager dog, a trim figure in gray snow pants, blue Search and Rescue parka and blue daypack, a bright knit cap over her dark hair. She looked very different from the dis-traught woman he had met in that hospital corridor two years before; competent and in control, a healthy flush in her cheeks and a brightness to her eyes that grief and frustration had drained away during her husband's illness.

She retrieved a half-empty paper coffee cup from the front of Diane's car, emptied the coffee and offered the cup to Jacquie to sniff. Then she and the dog disappeared down the trail, one of the other Search and Rescue volunteers jogging after them. Lucas returned to lean against his sheriff's department SUV to wait. The tall, thin volunteer walked over to join him. "Tony Meisner," the man introduced himself.

"Lucas Malone. I've only been here a week, on loan from Junction, and this is the second missing person's search I've been involved in. I'm beginning to wonder about this place."

Meisner, a lean man in his late thirties, leaned back next to Lucas against the patrol vehicle. "Maybe you're jinxing us. Though I can tell you from working search and rescue for fifteen years that calls tend to come in clusters. We'll get a trio of vehicle accidents or several falls in a row. This time it's missing persons, though let's hope this call has a happier ending than the last one."

"Did you know Dave Weiss?" Lucas asked.

"I did. We climbed together a few times, and we talked fishing whenever I went into his bakery."

"I didn't know him, but from what I've been told, he sounds like a great guy."

"He was."

"Did it surprise you that he'd take his own life?"

"They're sure it's suicide?" Tony asked.

"That seems to be the case. His wife said he was stressed lately."

"I wouldn't have said Dave would do something like that, but I guess you never know."

"Apparently, he was under a lot of financial stress."

"I didn't know that."

"When was the last time you saw him?" Lucas asked.

Tony rubbed his chin. "Saturday. I stopped in the bakery to get a loaf of sprouted grain bread and a bear claw."

"How did he seem?"

"I didn't actually talk to him. A teenager who works there part time waited on me. But Dave was there. I could see into the office he has behind the front counter. The door was open and he was arguing with someone. I didn't see who, and I only heard Dave's side of the conversation, but he was upset about something."

"You think he was arguing with someone?" Lucas asked. "What about?"

Tony shook his head. "I have no idea. I heard Dave say, 'No, that's not going to happen,' but then the clerk handed me my change and I left. Dave isn't the type to get angry easily, but he was really upset at whoever was in there."

A cheer rose up near the trailhead, and both men straightened as Anna and another woman emerged from the trail.

"Oh, I hate that you all had to come out here for me." Diane put her hands to her cheeks as she took in all the Search and Rescue volunteers gathered around her. "But I'm so glad you did." She turned to Anna. "And I'm so grateful to Anna and Jacquie for finding me."

"Are you all right?" Sheri asked.

"Oh, I'm fine," Diane said. She laughed. "Well, I'm looking forward to a nice hot shower, a glass of wine and dinner, but really, I'm fine. I was just foolish and got off the trail. I thought I could go around that snowslide and get back on the trail on the other side, but obviously I was wrong."

"She wasn't even that far from the trail when we found her," Anna said.

"Yes, but I didn't know that," Diane said. "I've hiked this trail half a dozen times, but everything looks different with all the snow."

"We're glad you're all right," Sheri said.

"Thank you all again, so much." Diane went around the group, shaking hands. She paused when she reached Lucas. "Oh, and the sheriff's department, too. I really have caused a lot of trouble."

"I'm glad you're okay." Lucas echoed the others. "Don't worry about the trouble. It's what we're here for."

"And I'm so grateful, really."

She moved on toward her Jeep and Lucas turned to Anna. "Good job," he said. "It didn't take you long to find her."

"Jacquie does all the work," she said. "I just follow her lead."

"I imagine it's nice to have a good outcome like this after what happened earlier in the week," he said.

"Oh, it is." She glanced around them then leaned in closer. "Have you learned any more about Dave's death?"

"The evidence points to a suicide," he said. "I'm sorry."

"What about the imprints from the ladder?" she asked.

"We don't know they were from a ladder, or when they were made," he said. "There's no indication that he had any enemies. His wife says he was upset enough about his financial situation to have killed himself."

"Yes, she told me the same thing." She hung her head.

"I'm sorry," he said. He wanted to put a hand on her shoulder to try to offer some comfort. But that wouldn't be appropriate.

"It's not your fault," she said.

"Still, I hate to see you so sad."

She raised her head and her eyes met his. "That's a very nice thing to say."

"Can I say something else?"

The pause was only as long as an inhale, but it felt much longer. "What do you want to say?" she asked at last.

"Will you have dinner with me?"

He had meant to say "coffee" or "a drink." Nothing as formal as dinner. He waited for her to say no, maybe even tell him he was way out of line. Instead, her cheeks flushed a little pinker and a dimple formed at the left side of her mouth. "Yes," she said. "Yes, I'd like that."

Chapter Five

Was this a date? Dinner was a date, right? But she didn't date. She wasn't ready to date. She felt too married to date. She wasn't married, of course. But she still felt that way, inside. She should call Lucas and say no. She could say something had come up. Or she could tell him she wasn't ready.

Anna paced back and forth across the bedroom, mind in turmoil. She couldn't remember the last time she had been so flustered. She forced herself to stop and take a deep breath. She had nothing to be nervous about. Nothing to feel guilty about. She could have dinner with a good-looking man who made her feel more like a woman than she had in over two years. There was nothing wrong with that, and maybe everything right.

Jacquie lay on the end of the bed, front paws neatly crossed at the wrists, intelligent brown eyes fixed on Anna. She sometimes wished the dog could talk, to render her opinion on the subject. She thought about calling Gemma, but Gemma would whoop and tell her it was about time she went out with someone, especially someone as good-looking as Lucas Malone.

Yes, he was handsome, but Anna didn't care about that. Or at least, it wasn't the most important thing. She wanted someone who had a good sense of humor. A man who was smart and kind. Lucas seemed like all of those things. And he had pointed out if they were going to have dinner together, she should stop addressing him as Deputy Malone. His first name, Lucas, felt a little awkward, but she was growing to like it.

"It's just one dinner," she said out loud. "It will be fine." But her stomach wobbled in a way that wasn't fine at all.

In the end, she managed to dress and do her hair and makeup in time to answer the doorbell when Lucas arrived. He wore the same black leather jacket she had seen him in before, but with black slacks, shined shoes and a blue button-down that made his eyes look even darker. "Hello," he said, and she felt the impact of his soft, deep voice, and the smile that went with it, just below her belly button.

They made small talk on the way to the restaurant, until after they had given their orders to the waiter. She began to relax. Lucas was easy to talk to. Why had she been so nervous?

"Do you know a man named Justin Trent?" he asked.

The water she had just sipped went down the wrong way and she started coughing. Several awkward moments passed before she could speak. "Justin is Jonas's brother," she said. "How do you know him?"

"He called me this morning."

"Why would Justin call you? He lives in Junction." And he definitely didn't know the two of them had agreed to go out.

"He wanted to know the cause of death for Dave Weiss. He said Dave was a friend and he had just learned he had died."

"Dave was Jonas's friend," she said. "Justin hardly knew him." She searched his face for some clue as to where this was leading. "What did you tell him?"

"I told him it looked like Dave had taken his own life."

"I told him that when I talked to him Wednesday," she said. "I don't know why he would call you. Maybe he didn't believe me." She took another sip of water, more cautious this time. "He always treats me as if I'm dim-witted. He thinks he knows what's best for everyone, including me."

"He said you had asked him a bunch of questions about some business deal Dave was involved in. He thought it might be a good idea for me to warn you not to interfere with a police investigation."

This time she was glad she wasn't trying to drink, or even holding a glass. "What did you say to that?"

"I told him you weren't interfering with anything."

The server arrived with their salads and she used the break in the conversation to try to think of what to say.

"I wasn't interfering," she said. "But Sandy told

me Dave had signed a contract with someone who distributes food to area restaurants. He agreed to buy desserts from Dave at a good price, and Dave invested in a new walk-in cooler and more help and equipment in anticipation of a big payoff. And I guess he owed this middleman commissions, too. But he didn't earn as much as he'd thought he would and the loans were at risk of being in default. Justin owns a restaurant in Junction and I thought he would know how an arrangement like that might work and could help me understand why Dave—who never showed any sign of wanting to expand the business or have more money—would have signed a contract with this guy."

He poured dressing onto his salad. "What did you find out?"

"Justin says there's a man named George Anton who acts as a middleman between small suppliers and restaurants. He pays good prices to the suppliers and offers competitive prices to the restaurants. Justin said Anton supplies some items for Red Mesa, Justin's restaurant. Then he made some snide remark about how I shouldn't be playing amateur detective. Which was bad enough, but to have him call you is infuriating."

"I'm impressed," Lucas said. "You found out a lot more than I knew about. Sandy didn't give me any particulars about Dave's business dealings. She just said they owed a lot of money he realized he couldn't pay back."

"If I was her, I'd be frantic right now about that

debt," Anna said. "But Sandy was perfectly calm. She said she'd let that loan default and move on."

"Do you think she'll continue to operate the bakery?"

"I would have thought so. I knew Dave was the original baker, but my impression was that she helped a lot. And he told me when he catered our wedding that Sandy did most of the decorating. He said she was the more artistic of the two of them. Still, maybe the work was too much for her on her own, and she didn't want to hire someone to take Dave's place. I can see how that would be awkward." She stabbed at her salad. "Apparently, both the bakery and her home are up for sale."

"Maybe she's not as blasé about the debt as you think," Lucas said. "Maybe she needs to sell the house and the bakery right away to pay off the loans her husband took out."

"I'm really surprised Dave ended up in such a fix in the first place," she said. "He was never one of these people who is always out for more, looking for new ways to bring in more money. He and Jonas were alike that way—not exactly unambitious, but content to keep their businesses smaller. 'Manageable,' Jonas used to say."

"What kind of business did your husband have?" Lucas asked.

"He owned a small construction company. He built custom homes mostly, and did some remodeling." She pushed lettuce around the plate. "He had people who worked for him, but really, the business was all about him and his leadership and skills. Without him, there really was no business."

"So you decided to open your own business?"

She shook her head. "No. At first I thought I'd get a job working for someone else. I had done all the bookkeeping, payroll, etcetera, for Jonas for the past few years, so I started applying to offices around town. I got one job offer from a man I didn't particularly like, another builder in town. The pay he offered wasn't really enough to live on. I could have supplemented my paycheck with Jonas's life insurance money, but the whole idea of the job depressed me. I was walking back to my car after the job interview and I saw the For Lease sign in the window of the building that houses my shop. I'd thought about doing something like this for years and I figured, why not now?"

"And it's worked out for you?"

"It has." She smiled, happy to talk about something that had become so precious to her. "I look forward to going into the store every day and I've made some wonderful friends."

"It's good to hear you're doing so well. I bet your husband would be pleased."

She tried to hide her disappointment in his remark. So far they had talked about her husband's brother, her husband's friend and now her husband himself. Lucas didn't sound like someone who was interested in any kind of romantic relationship. "I have no idea what Jonas would think," she said. "He liked having me working for him. I liked it, too, but the few times I talked about doing something with my knitting—opening an Etsy shop, for example— he wasn't exactly encouraging. I think he saw knitting as a quirky little hobby, not a real business."

Opening Yarn and More and making it a success was the first thing she had done solely for herself since her marriage. Along with pride in her accomplishment came so many other emotions—sadness, guilt, regret. She shook her head and pushed aside her half-eaten salad. She didn't want to go there. Not tonight. This was supposed to be a time for her and Lucas to get to know each other better. At least, that was how she had viewed the evening.

"Are you enjoying your stay in Eagle Mountain?" she asked.

"It's a beautiful place," he said. "I've been here a number of times before. Junction is only a little over an hour away, after all."

"Have you lived in Junction long?"

"Seven years. I moved there from Fort Collins after I graduated from the state's police academy. Jenny, my girlfriend, moved over about a year later."

Their entrées arrived and Anna wrestled with what to say next. Were they going to talk about his girlfriend now? She was curious about the woman who had apparently been dying about the same time as Jonas. Such an odd thing for the two of them to have in common and yet there was comfort in knowing he probably understood a lot of what she had gone through. Why not let him know that she could empathize with him? "You had been together quite a while, then," she said. As long as she was married to Jonas.

"We were." He looked even sadder.

"There are so many emotions to process," she said. "Grief, of course, but also guilt."

He leaned toward her. "You feel guilty?"

She nodded. "I think everyone who is left behind feels that way. Sandy is probably feeling it now. I always wondered if I had urged Jonas to go to the doctor sooner, or if we had eaten healthier, could I have saved him? The answer is probably no, but still, we torture ourselves with questions like that."

He sat back. "I guess so." He seemed to gather himself and his expression took on a new warmth. "I'm sure Jonas knew how much you loved him. How devoted you were. You should take comfort from that."

She nodded and neither of them spoke for a long moment, but in the silence there was closeness— she had seldom talked to someone who knew so intimately what she had gone through.

After a moment, he touched her hand and smiled. She felt the heat of that look all the way to her toes. "I'm feeling better about life in general these days," he said. "What about you?"

She returned the smile. "'Life goes on' sounds so trite," she said. "But it's true. I remember the first day I woke up and felt excited about the day ahead. I felt lighter. Not exactly happy, but not depressed, either, as if a cloud had lifted. Of course, the next day I cried half the day, but it was one baby step forward and then there were others. Now, most days, I feel pretty good. I can see possibilities again, and that's such a relief."

He nodded and cut into his chicken. "You're in a good place—your own house, friends, a business you love. And, hey, if the yarn store doesn't work out, you could always be an amateur detective. You seem pretty good at it." He winked and she burst out laughing. Their eyes met and she felt lit from within.

From that moment on, the evening changed, as if, having acknowledged the ghosts of their pasts, they were ready to focus on this moment. She told him about training Jacquie to be a search dog, volunteering with Search and Rescue, and about some of their adventures. He shared amusing encounters he had had as a law enforcement officer, including retrieving a marmot that had hitched a ride in a tourist's SUV from a high-mountain parking area to downtown Junction.

"I decided right then I'd never make it as a wildlife officer," he said. "The ungrateful little rodent bit me and I worried I'd have to get rabies shots, but the doctor finally decided that wasn't necessary."

"The poor thing was probably frightened," she said.

"He wasn't the only one. You think they're cute when you see them on the side of the road, but up close, in a confined space, they look twice as big and fierce."

She laughed more than she could remember laughing in two years. When the server asked for the third time if they needed anything else, she looked across at him and felt grateful and happy—and definitely attracted. "We'd probably better go," he said.

She nodded and they stood and collected their coats. He slid hers onto her shoulder, his fingertips lightly brushing her collarbone as he did so, sending a hot tremor through her.

He drove back to her house in comfortable silence, music playing softly on the radio. At one point, he reached across and took her hand and she didn't pull away. She felt closer to him than she could have imagined she would to someone she had known such a short time.

Then again, she could say she had known him for two years. They hadn't been together during that time but, for a while, they had led parallel lives, each dealing with one of the worst things a person could go through. That made for a kind of kinship most people would never have.

He parked in her driveway and they got out. She debated whether or not to invite him in, and what kind of message that sent. In front of her door, the light she had left on bathed them both in a golden glow. He leaned closer. "Is it okay if I kiss you good night?" he asked.

She nodded, suddenly tongue-tied. She was about to tell him it was more than okay, but his lips covered hers, sending a thrilling heat all the way through her. She gripped his shoulders and arched up toward him, and he wrapped his arm around her and drew her close. She opened her mouth and his tongue teased

across her lips. It had been a long time since she had
been kissed this way, and she realized how much she
had missed. Missed this physical surge of pleasure
and the sensation of being someone's complete focus.
Missed the tingle of desire that made her feel giddy
and daring. Missed the anticipation of what might
come next. Something good.

She would ask him inside, she decided. Reckless.
But she wasn't an unsure girl. She didn't have to wonder what he'd think of her or care what the neighbors would say. Life was short and they both knew
that better than most. Why not enjoy whatever they
could, right now?

They parted, both breathing hard, and she smiled
and started to turn toward the door, but a movement
over his right shoulder made her gasp. She pulled back
and he whirled around, pushing her behind him, shielding her with his body. "Who's there?" he demanded.

Sandy Weiss moved out of the shadows into the
path of the porch light. "It's just me." She smirked.
"Sorry to interrupt."

Anna pressed a hand to her chest, trying to slow
the racing of her heart. "Sandy, what are you doing
here?"

"I wanted to talk to you."

"You have my phone number, don't you?"

"This wasn't something I wanted to talk about on
the phone." She looked at Lucas.

"I'll go," he said, but made no move to leave.

"You can stay," Sandy said. "Maybe you need to
hear this, too."

"What are you talking about?" Anna asked. "You're scaring me."

"Could we go inside? It's cold out here. Besides, I don't like being out here where anyone can see us together."

"Of course." Anna pulled her key from her purse. "But give me some idea of what has you so frightened."

"I'm not frightened!" She sounded angry. "I'm just being smart."

"What are you being smart about?" Lucas asked.

Sandy ignored him, her focus still on Anna. "I'm beginning to wonder if you were right the first time," she said.

"Right about what?" Anna fit the key in the lock and turned it.

"Maybe Dave didn't kill himself. Because now I think someone is trying to kill me."

Chapter Six

Lucas followed the two women into the house. While Anna greeted the dog and switched on lights, Sandy shrugged out of her parka and settled onto the sofa. The room's furnishings were simple and homey, with a braided rug on the hardwood floor and furniture upholstered in brown or soft blue. A knitted throw in those same colors draped across the back of one of two armchairs. "Can I get you anything?" Anna asked. "A glass of water, or I could make coffee or tea."

"Always the perfect hostess." Sandy shook her head. "Don't you want to hear what happened?"

Anna sat at the opposite end of the sofa. "Of course."

Lucas took the chair across from the women, the one with the blanket. "What makes you think someone is trying to kill you?" he asked.

Sandy crossed and uncrossed her legs. She was dressed in jeans, a gray sweatshirt with Downtown Gym in black letters across the chest, hiking boots and a black fleece beanie pulled over her short blond hair. Dark shadows beneath her eyes testified to sleepless nights. "It started with phone calls," she said.

"The first one came the afternoon after Dave's body was found. Someone called the bakery and, when I answered, a man said, 'Keep your mouth shut or you're next' and hung up."

"Did you recognize the voice?" Lucas asked.

"No. It was very deep. Really, it sounded like someone trying to make his voice deeper."

"Did you contact the sheriff's office?" Lucas asked.

"No, why would I? It was just some creep."

"You said 'phone calls,'" Lucas said. "There was more than one?"

"Yes. I got another call the next morning with the same message." She shifted on the sofa, as if trying to get more comfortable. "And one that afternoon. That third time, I told the caller to get lost, though I didn't use such polite language. No calls today, so I figure that solved the problem."

"Now you don't think so?" Anna asked.

"No. Because this evening I got this." She leaned onto one hip, pulled something out of the back pocket of her jeans and handed it to Anna. Anna unfolded a piece of paper, read it, then passed it to Lucas.

He studied a sheet of lined notebook paper, the ragged left edge indicating it had been torn from a spiral notebook, with pasted-on letters that appeared to be cut from a magazine that read "Keep your mouth shut or you'll end up like your husband." He looked up at Sandy. "Keep your mouth shut about what?"

"I have no idea," she said. "It's silly, really." She

glanced at Anna. "But then I started thinking about what you said about Dave's body being so high up in that tree, and how you had seen what looked like marks from a ladder. I wanted to talk to you and see if you really thought that meant that Dave didn't kill himself."

"Mrs. Weiss, do you believe your husband was involved in something that could have gotten him killed?" Lucas asked.

She turned to him, fine lines on her high forehead. "I don't," she said. "I thought Dave was on edge because of the money we owed, but what if that wasn't it? What if he was so stressed because someone was threatening him?"

"Have you found anything to indicate that was the case—any notes your husband received similar to this one?" He tapped the paper in his hand.

"No. And Dave never said anything. But he wouldn't have wanted to worry me."

She wouldn't be the first spouse who was in the dark about her partner's business affairs—legal or illegal. "I spoke with someone who said they came into the bakery last Saturday and heard your husband arguing with someone in his office," Lucas told her. "The customer couldn't see who the person was, but they said Dave was very upset. Do you know who that was?"

She pressed her lips together. "Last Saturday morning or afternoon?" she asked after a pause.

"Afternoon."

She shook her head. "I have no idea. I wasn't at the bakery then."

"You have someone who works for you?"

Sandy nodded. "Ashley Dietrich. She's a high school student. But I don't think Dave would argue with her. She's such a timid kid. She would crumple if you raised your voice at her."

"When does she work her next shift?" Lucas asked.

"I had to let her go. I can't afford to keep an employee with Dave gone. I'll handle things myself for now."

Lucas made a note in his book. "This person said they heard your husband tell the other person 'No, that's not going to happen.'"

Sandy relaxed a little. "Dave was probably on the phone. And I'm pretty sure he was talking with George Anton. That's the restaurant supplier we agreed to sell desserts to. But they weren't arguing. They were just discussing the next delivery. This customer—whoever it was—must have misunderstood." She turned to Anna again. "You know Dave. He never got angry with anyone. That wasn't like him."

Tony Meisner had said he could see Dave and he was sure he was talking to another person, not on the phone. Tony hadn't struck Lucas as the type to exaggerate or misinterpret. "If your husband didn't kill himself, do you have any idea who was responsible for his death?" he asked.

Sandy held out both hands, palms up. "No idea at all." She leaned toward him. "Do you think he was murdered?"

"If this was a random crime, the killer went to a lot of trouble, going to that remote location, hauling out a ladder and rope, and your husband," he said. "Suicide seems more likely."

"If someone murdered Dave, you need to find out who," she said.

"You said you believed your husband was upset enough about his financial problems to kill himself," Lucas reminded her.

"I don't think that anymore. Not after these threats."

"We can see about getting you into a safe house," Lucas said. "Someplace whoever is threatening you won't be able to reach you."

"Oh, no, I'm not going anywhere." Sandy crossed her arms over her chest. "I have a business to run. I need to plan Dave's funeral. I'm not going to hide. You just do your job and find whoever is doing this."

"We'll certainly look into the matter," Lucas said. "We can start by examining your phone records. Maybe we can track the caller."

The lines on her forehead deepened. "You can really do that? Our bakery gets dozens of calls a day and we don't have caller ID or anything."

"It will help if you can remember what time the calls came in."

"The closest I can get is morning or afternoon." She leaned toward him. "My husband died. I'm going to have to sell my home and my business. I'm not sleeping. I don't know whether I'm coming or going. Grief does that to you, you know?"

He knew. "We'll do the best we can," he said.

"Is there anything else you can think of that might help? Anything your husband said to you? Anyone who was angry with him about anything? A former employee who left unhappy? A customer?"

She shook her head. "Nothing like that. Dave was a really nice guy. If anything, he was too nice. I always worried about people taking advantage of him."

"What do you mean?"

"Nothing important," she said. "You know, if someone complained they didn't like the pie they bought, Dave just automatically refunded their money. He didn't argue or ask questions or anything. He'd stay late to fill an order for someone who waited until the last minute to call. He let people take advantage of him like that."

"Everybody liked Dave." Anna hadn't spoken for so long, the sound of her voice seemed to startle Sandy. "I never heard anyone say a word against him."

Right. The man was a saint. But if Sandy was right, someone had disliked him enough to kill him.

"Sandy, you're welcome to spend the night here," Anna said. "You can stay as long as you need to, while the sheriff's department checks out these threats."

"I'll be fine in my own home." Sandy stood. "I'm not the skittish type."

Lucas stood and followed Sandy to the door. "I'll follow you home, just to make sure you arrive safely," he said.

"Aren't you the gentleman?" Sandy looked him

up and down then glanced at Anna. "I'll wait in my car while you say good night," she said.

ANNA TOLD HERSELF she should be grateful for this offer of privacy, but the smirk that accompanied the words spoiled the mood. Lucas waited until the door had closed behind Sandy before he turned to her. "I'm sorry to leave you like this," he said. "But I really should make sure everything is all right at Sandy's house."

"Of course you should." She forced a smile. "It's getting late anyway."

"Dinner was nice," he said.

"Yes." She couldn't meet his gaze. She had been feeling a lot bolder until Sandy showed up. Now she felt awkward and unsure.

Lucas touched her shoulder. "Good night."

She lifted her gaze to his. "Good night," she said then, impulsively, she leaned forward and hastily kissed his cheek. She pulled away. "You'd better go. Sandy will be getting impatient."

He let himself out and she waited until she heard both vehicles drive away before she sat on the sofa again. Jacquie jumped up beside her and laid her head in Anna's lap. "I don't know if I'm ready for this, girl," she said as she massaged the dog's ears. Being on her own was easier, and she had thought she was happy that way. But now she had a good-looking, interesting, intelligent man who seemed interested in her as well. Being alone didn't seem so happy, after all, but opening herself up to someone else felt pretty scary. "Unlike Sandy, I guess I am the skittish sort," she said.

Jacquie whined and Anna went to the back door and let her out then, instead of following the dog, she opened the door into the garage. She flipped on the light and studied the tarp-covered shape that filled half the space next to her Outback. Jacquie came to sit beside her, and let out a low whine.

Anna walked around her car and lifted the tarp. Beneath it, the 1974 Dodge Dart was a patchwork of Bondo, primer and remnants of the original red paint, now oxidized and nicked. A dusty collection of parts salvaged from junkyards around the state filled the front and back seats of the vehicle, which Jonas always referred to as "The Dart" as if it were the only one ever made. It was the only one for him anyway. He'd also called it "my baby" and she'd known he wasn't even joking.

After he'd died, Anna had donated his clothing and sold his tools, but she hadn't been able to part with the Dart. He had spent so much time with it, invested so much of himself into it, how could she let it go?

Minutes ticked by as she stared at the car, trying to picture Jonas bent over the engine, singing off-key to country radio as he worked. In the early days after he'd died, it was as if his ghost haunted this space. She had been able to see him here. To hear him. But not in a while.

She lowered the tarp and smoothed it over the fender,

then turned to go back inside. Time for bed. Alone. No new lover and no ghosts to keep her company.

ASHLEY DIETRICH WAS a slight, pale, sixteen-year-old who told Lucas she had worked for the bakery for three months. She sat on the sofa next to her mother, who had somewhat reluctantly agreed to the deputy's request to interview her daughter before Ashley left for her new part-time job Saturday morning. Ashley tucked her long, strawberry-blond hair behind one ear and stared down at the chipped red polish on her nails. "Mrs. W. told me a couple of days ago that she's planning on closing down the place since Mr. W. died, so I had to find another job."

She looked up at Lucas, light green eyes wide. "That sounded terrible, didn't it? I didn't mean that. I'm really sorry Mr. W. died. He was a super nice guy. He was always thanking me and telling me I was doing a good job." She bit her lower lip. "This was my first job and I was really nervous, but he made it easy."

"I want to ask you about the Saturday before Dave Weiss died," Lucas said. "That would be Saturday, March 12. You worked that morning, is that correct?"

Ashley nodded. "I worked every Saturday. Seven a.m. to three p.m."

"That afternoon, you waited on Tony Meisner," Lucas said. "Do you remember him?"

Ashley's brow furrowed. "He's a regular customer. He bought a bear claw. And maybe a loaf of bread?" Her voice rose in question.

"That's right. Tony said while he was in the store, he heard Mr. Weiss in his office, arguing with someone. Who came to the bakery to see him that afternoon?"

"No one came to see Mr. W. that afternoon," Ashley said. "It was just me and him and Mrs. W. there all day. And she was only there for a couple of hours. She had fire department stuff to do, or something like that."

"Could someone have come in a back door to the office?" Lucas asked.

"There isn't a back door to the office," Ashley said. "There's a door on the loading dock, but that goes right into the freezer, from when the building was a meat market, so it doesn't get used much, though they keep flour and stuff in the freezer. The only way into the office is through the front door and behind the counter."

"Could someone have come in while you were away, maybe using the restroom or something?"

"I guess. But I would have heard them in there with Mr. W. He never closed the door or anything."

Tony had told Lucas the door was open and he could see Dave. Maybe he had the day wrong. "Did you ever hear Mr. Weiss argue with someone when you were at the bakery?" he asked.

"You mean besides his wife?" She blushed. "I mean, it's not like they fought all the time, but they did have some, um, loud conversations when I was working."

Everyone had painted a picture of Sandy and Dave

as devoted to each other, but Lucas wasn't really surprised to hear they hadn't always gotten along. Every couple rubbed each other the wrong way from time to time, and he would imagine it could be even worse if you not only lived but worked together. "What did they argue about?" he asked.

Ashley shrugged. "The foolish stuff people fight about," she said. "She thought he was careless about picking up his clothes off the floor or paying bills. He thought she was too uptight about money."

"Do you remember any specific argument?" Lucas asked.

"No. I really didn't pay attention. I mean, why would I?"

Why would a teenager care about an older married couple's squabbles? "Thanks, Ashley. Just one more question. Do you think Mr. Weiss was worried about anything before he died?"

"You mean, like, was he upset enough about something to kill himself?" She shook her head, the large gold hoops in her ears swaying with the movement. "I was really surprised when I heard what happened. He was a really upbeat kind of guy. Not the type to stress over stuff. I dropped a whole box of cupcakes one time and I was sure he'd fire me, or at least yell at me for being clumsy. Instead, he helped me pick up everything and made a joke about how he was glad he wasn't the only person in the shop who was a klutz." She dabbed at a tear in the corner of her eye. "I can't imagine how much he must have been hurting inside to go and hang himself. It's terrible."

Mrs. Dietrich handed her daughter a tissue from a box on the coffee table between them. "It's almost time for Ashley to leave for work," she said.

Lucas stood. "Thank you for talking to me, Ashley," he said.

Mrs. Dietrich walked Lucas to the door. "What is this about?" she whispered. "Is there something going on besides Dave Weiss killing himself?"

"I'm just getting a better picture of his last days," Lucas said.

She frowned but didn't say anything more.

Lucas checked his watch. He had a few minutes before he had to be at a meeting at the sheriff's department. His conversation with Ashley hadn't provided any new information, though it had added another name to the list of people who were surprised to learn Dave Weiss had taken his own life. He had thought finding the person Dave had argued with that Saturday might lead to a reason for Dave's suicide, or a suspect in his murder, but maybe Sandy was right and Dave had been having a phone conversation with George Anders.

He made a note to call Anders and set up an interview. His name kept popping up in this investigation, one more piece of the puzzle Lucas needed to complete the picture of Dave Weiss's final days.

Chapter Seven

Saturday morning, Anna had scarcely set her mug of coffee on the worktable when Gemma pounced, "I ordered take-out from Mad Thai last night. When Terry went to pick it up, he said he saw you and some really good-looking guy having dinner. He said the two of you looked really cozy."

"Did Terry really say he was good-looking?"

Gemma's husband could have posed for photos as a "mountain man" with big biceps and a bigger beard. Anna had never seen him in anything but jeans and a plaid flannel shirt and work boots. He drove a pickup truck with oversized tires, owned a hunting dog named Minnie and had visibly paled and then refused when Gemma had asked him to hold her purse while she went into the ladies' room at a local music festival.

"No, but he said the guy was about your age, had really dark hair and looked fit—that sounds like good-looking to me." She slid into the chair across from Anna. "Was it that new sheriff's deputy who was in here the other day? He had really dark hair and I thought he was really into you."

"You saw the man for all of five minutes." Anna shifted, pinned by Gemma's avid interest. "You couldn't possibly tell something like that."

"It was him, wasn't it?" Gemma said. "I can tell because you're blushing."

"I am not." Anna put one hand to her hot cheek. Good thing she had never aspired to the stage—she was a terrible actor.

"Liar." Gemma laughed. "And I guess all those excuses you made about not being ready to date were lies, too."

"I wasn't lying," Anna protested. "Not intentionally anyway. This just…happened."

Gemma leaned closer. "Tell me all about the deputy. What is his name again?"

"Lucas. Lucas Malone."

"He even has a sexy name. So, you had dinner, then what?"

"Then we went back to my house to talk."

Gemma raised both eyebrows. "Did you really just talk or is that a euphemism for something else?"

"When we got to my house, Sandy Weiss was there, waiting for us."

Gemma sat back, eyebrows in their normal position now. "What was Sandy doing there?"

"Apparently, she got some threatening phone calls and a note. She's wondering if the same person was threatening Dave. And maybe he didn't really kill himself."

"You mean he was murdered?" Gemma popped out of the chair then sat again, as if she couldn't quite contain her excitement. "But Sandy said it was suicide, right? Because Dave was having money problems?"

"She said that, but now she's not sure." Anna sipped the coffee, trying to organize her thoughts. "You knew Dave. He wasn't the brooding type. As far as I know, he had no history of depression. And so many things about that scene by the river seemed so odd."

"It did seem like a lot of trouble to go to," Gemma said. "Dave never struck me as one for making a production of anything. Sandy was the drama queen in that relationship."

"Do you think so?" Anna asked. Sandy had always struck her as blunt, quick to anger maybe and even cynical, but not one for hysterics or exaggeration.

"Trust me, I've known Sandy since she was a teenager. She was one of the popular girls, and she used to go on and on about how she was going to marry a rich guy and live in a mansion in California and have a great tan while the rest of us shoveled snow all winter. I was pretty surprised when she ended up marrying one of her fellow firefighters. Dave was a great guy, but he never had that kind of ambition."

"They were wild about each other," Anna said. "I know losing him has been so hard on her."

"And now someone's threatening her," Gemma said. "What kind of threats?"

"Nothing specific. Just 'keep your mouth shut or else.'"

"Shut about what?"

"She doesn't know, and I believe her."

"Yeah, I doubt the wife of a bakery owner in a small town knows anything most people would care about," Gemma said.

They turned as the bells on the front door announced a customer.

Lucas stopped just inside the door. He wore his khaki sheriff's department uniform, starched creases and very official-looking. Very handsome. Her stomach fluttered as his eyes met hers.

"Good morning, Deputy," Gemma called, breaking the spell. She grinned and gave Anna a thumbs-up. Anna shooed the gesture away.

"Hello, Lucas. What can we do for you this morning?" She stood and went to meet him.

"I need to ask a couple more questions," he said.

"Sure." She looked around. There were no customers in the store but one could arrive any minute. "We can go back to the store room."

"Don't bother," Gemma said. "I have a sudden urge to walk down the street and get another cup of coffee." She stood and hurried out the front door before Anna could protest.

Anna turned back to Lucas. "What is it you need to ask me?"

"Did Dave and Sandy ever have a dog?"

She frowned. "I don't think so. Maybe before I

met them, and for a few years they had a cat. Sparky. They haven't had a pet at all for a while now."

"Any friends or neighbors with dogs who have seizures?"

She stared at him. "I don't know. What is this about?"

He winced. "It's confidential."

"Does this have something to do with Dave's death? Are you thinking now it isn't suicide?"

He moved closer and lowered his voice. "You can't tell anyone."

"Of course not. I wouldn't."

"The autopsy found a sedative in Dave's blood. A drug that is used to control seizures in dogs."

"Somebody killed him with dog meds?"

"No. He died because of the hanging. He may have even taken the drug himself, to calm down and make what he was going to do easier."

"Maybe you should talk to the local vet," she said. "There probably aren't that many dogs around here on that drug."

"I have an appointment with the vet's office this afternoon," he said.

"How is Sandy doing?" Anna asked. "I mean, how did she seem when you left her last night?"

"Tense, exhausted. About like you would expect. But she's determined to stay in her own home. She seemed more annoyed by the threats than frightened."

"Have you found out any more about those threats?"

He hesitated.

"Tell me," she said. "I already know one big se-cret. I promise I can keep the rest. I found him, re-member? And Dave was my friend. I'm not just asking because I'm nosy."

"We were able to identify three calls about the times Sandy reported receiving the threats," he said. "They were all from an untraceable cell phone. One of those pay-as-you-go things you can buy at gas sta-tions and other stores."

"A burner phone!" She flushed. "Sorry. I like de-tective fiction."

"We're not going to have any luck tracking down that phone," he said. "I stopped by the bakery just now and told her we need to look at her husband's computer. She said he didn't have a laptop. There's just the computer at work."

"What about his phone?" Anna asked.

"Dave's phone?"

"I don't remember him having a laptop, but he did everything on his phone. Have you found it?"

"No. Sandy said she didn't know where it was. I thought he might have pitched it into the pond be-fore he killed himself."

"Or his killer has it."

"We can try to trace it." He made a note. "Thanks." He looked up.

"Anything else you want to tell me?" she asked.

"Just that I'd like to see you again. Though I'm not sure when. This investigation is probably going to require overtime."

"I'd like to go out with you again," she said. "But

finding out what really happened to Dave is more important."

"We still can't rule out suicide," Lucas said.

"I know. But you can't let a killer go unpunished, either."

"No," he agreed. "And I want to stop whoever it is before they hurt Sandy. It would help if we could figure out who would benefit from his death. Not Sandy—she still has to deal with the debts Dave left behind. He had a small life insurance policy, but it's not a big payout." He scanned his notebook again. "I know Dave owned a bakery. Were there any competing businesses, someone who would gain by killing off the competition?"

"I think one bakery is about all Eagle Mountain can support," she said. "It helped that Dave had such a good reputation in the area. He catered weddings and things like that."

He nodded. "I know these questions might seem random, but with so little to go on, I'm trying to look at every angle."

"I understand. If I think of anything useful, I'll let you know." She glanced over in time to see Gemma peering in the front window. When Gemma realized she had been caught, she straightened and hurried away.

"I'd better go." Lucas touched her arm. "I'm glad I got a chance to see you again."

"Me, too." She couldn't hold back a smile, though she felt a little foolish, so giddy over a man she scarcely knew.

She walked with him to the door, but as they reached it, her phone alerted her to a text message and his shoulder-mounted radio crackled. She stepped away to read her message while he responded to the dispatcher.

"I've got to report to a traffic accident near Dakota Ridge," he said.

"So do I. Search and Rescue says there are two people trapped in the car."

"Do they need a search dog for that?" he asked.

"No, but I volunteer with Search and Rescue as more than a search dog handler. They were recruiting volunteers last fall and I already knew everyone and I thought, *Why not? I'm learning a lot.*"

"You're pretty amazing," he said.

"I don't know about that." She pocketed the phone. "We'd better go."

"Can I give you a ride?" he asked.

She shook her head. "I need to get to Search and Rescue headquarters, but I'll see you there."

IN HIS TIME in the mountains, Lucas had seen many similar motor vehicle accidents. Drivers going too fast, not paying attention, or simply unlucky enough to meet with bad road conditions, went off the side of a steep pass. Sometimes the cars rolled. Sometimes they crashed on rocks or hung up on trees. Sometimes drivers or their passengers died, but he had seen many survivors, too.

He didn't yet know the fate of the occupants of the black Escalade on its side in the river below Dakota

Ridge. He met up with the driver who had called in the accident and they stood on the side of the road, looking down on the wreck. "I think he must have hit a patch of ice," the caller, a slight man in his fifties, wispy blond-white hair combed over a pink scalp, said. He twisted his hands together and made a clicking noise with his tongue against his teeth. "I sure hope they're not dead."

They both turned at the sound of an approaching vehicle to see the orange Search and Rescue Jeep pull in behind Lucas's cruiser. The SAR volunteers, including Anna, piled out. She had changed into technical pants and boots, and a blue Eagle Mountain Search and Rescue parka. SAR captain Sherri Stevens and volunteer Tony Meisner joined Lucas and the caller, who introduced himself as Alex. "Have you heard any cries for help or anything like that?" Sheri asked.

They both shook their heads. "All right," Sheri said. "We'll take it from here."

Lucas collected Alex's contact information and told him he could leave. "Is it okay if I stick around?" he asked. "I want to know what happened to the people in the car."

"All right, but you'll need to stay back, out of the way."

"No problem." Alex retreated to his car, where he stood and peered down at the scene below.

Rescuers were already running rope lines and making their way down toward the Escalade. Two men secured the vehicle with chains and blocks, then two other volunteers with full packs followed. Sheri directed the others to ready a litter and handle more ropes. Anna moved with assurance among the tangle of people and equipment, kneeling to help with one task then moving to the next.

Down at the Escalade, the two first responders with the packs leaned into the vehicle. They managed to wrench the passenger's-side door open and the smaller of the two climbed in. Then both swarmed into the cab.

"Two people, a man and a woman, both alive and responsive," Sheri announced. The radio in her hand beeped again and she listened intently. Lucas moved closer and heard the crunch of Alex's footsteps behind him.

"The female passenger has multiple cuts and a possible broken forearm," came the message over the radio. "The driver is dazed, after apparently hitting his head. No other obvious injuries. We'll need litters to bring both of them up."

The team went into action once more. Some volunteers rigged more lines, while others climbed down with two metal litters and a variety of medical gear. Anna worked with Tony, rigging one set of lines. In the canyon, volunteers fitted the driver and passenger with neck and back braces, then gently moved them from the vehicle onto the ground, where they conducted more examinations. They eased the woman onto a large orange air mattress then lifted the mattress into one of the litters. She was strapped in and fitted with a helmet like the ones the volunteers wore. The litter was attached to a line and the slow climb toward the top began.

The man, whom Lucas judged to be in his forties, had dark hair and a middleweight boxer's build. He loudly protested that he could walk, but he was coaxed into the litter and he, too, was carried to the top with a volunteer walking on either side of the litter.

"The ambulance is on its way to transport these two." Sheri joined Lucas beside his cruiser, where he had retreated to be out of the way. After hearing that the two people in the car were alive, Alex had driven away. "The man's name is George Anton. The woman with him is Shaylin Brown. He says he wasn't driving too fast. He hit a patch of ice and the Escalade went flying."

"George Anton?" Lucas confirmed.

"Yeah. Do you know him? He said he was from Junction."

"Not exactly."

A cheer rose up as the stretcher with Ms. Brown reached the top. Anna hurried to unfasten the litter from the ropes and then helped carry the injured woman to a level patch of ground. A second group of volunteers worked to do the same with George, though he insisted on being allowed to sit up on the litter once it was on a level patch of mud and snow.

Lucas approached the man. "Mr. Anton?" he asked.

The man looked up at Lucas with sad brown eyes. "Don't tell me you're going to give me a ticket," he said. "I didn't do anything wrong. It was the ice. Why do they even keep this road open in winter if it's so dangerous?"

"No ticket." Lucas squatted down until he was eye-level with Anton. "Where were you headed when you hit the ice?" he asked.

"I was coming from a meeting with a client in Eagle Mountain, on my way to meet a different client in Paradise."

"Who did you meet with in Eagle Mountain?"

"Why are you asking?"

Lucas shrugged. "It's a small town. I'm just curious."

"Her name is Sandy Weiss. You know her?"

Lucas thought he did a good job of hiding his surprise. "She and her husband have the bakery."

"That's right. I'm a restaurant supplier and I get some of my desserts from the Weisses. Here." He dug in his pocket and pulled out a business card. "Anton's Finest—restaurant provisions. Local products are our specialty."

"You know Dave Weiss died last Sunday," Lucas said. "His body was found Monday."

"I heard. It's a terrible shame, but Sandy called and asked me to meet her. She wants to make sure we're on the same page."

"I understood you dealt mainly with Dave Weiss before."

Anton gave him a long, considering look. "It doesn't matter now because he's dead, so she's the one I deal with."

"Who is the woman with you?" Lucas asked.

"Shaylin. She works with me. I thought it would be good to have a woman along when I spoke to Sandy. In case things got emotional, you know?" He pulled out his phone. "I need to call my client in Paradise and let him know we're not going to make it." He swore. "There's no signal." He shook his phone. "What's wrong with this thing?"

"There's no signal right here," Lucas said. One of many dead spots in this remote mountainous area.

"Mr. Anton?" Sheri approached them, a paramedic beside her. "This is Emmett. He's going to check you out then take you to the hospital." Nearby, another volunteer and a paramedic examined Ms. Brown.

Several minutes later, as the ambulance pulled away, Anna came to stand beside Lucas. "I think they're both going to be all right," she said.

"Did you know that was George Anton?"

She stared. "The man Sandy talked about? The one who contracted with Dave to supply restaurants with baked goods?"

"Yes. He said he was on his way from a meeting with Sandy when his car went off the road."

"Who was the woman with him?"

"Her name is Shaylin Brown. He said she works with him."

Anna sucked in her breath. The sound made him look at her more closely. "Do you know her?" he asked.

She shook her head. "It's probably someone else

with the same name. You did say Shaylin, right? Not Sheila or Sharon?"

"Shaylin. It's not a very common name. Who is the woman you know?"

She blew out a breath and gave him a rueful look. "She's Justin's mistress."

Chapter Eight

Lucas stared at Anna. "Justin Trent, your brother-in-law, the restaurant owner?"

She nodded. "Not long before Jonas died, Gloria, Justin's wife, got a call from a woman named Shaylin Brown. The woman said she and Justin had been lovers for two years and Gloria needed to do the right thing and give Justin the divorce he wanted. Gloria said she was completely blindsided. She had no idea anything was wrong and Justin had never mentioned divorce. She was devastated, and when Jonas found out, he was furious."

"What happened after that?" Lucas asked.

"Justin groveled and begged Gloria to take him back. He quit seeing Shaylin—or at least he says he did—and he and Gloria went to counseling. But none of that happened until after Jonas died. Maybe I'm being petty, but I'm still angry about that. Jonas was really upset about the affair, and knowing Justin was doing the right thing would have made him so happy." Her eyes met his. "He didn't have much to be happy about in those last weeks."

He nodded and looked away, giving her time to pull herself together.

"Justin said he and Shaylin worked together," she said after a moment. "I always thought it meant she worked at the restaurant, but maybe they met because she worked for George Anton."

"You said it's been two years. Maybe Justin fired her, or she quit when he ended the affair, and she went to work for Anton then."

"Do you think he was in Eagle Mountain to put pressure on Sandy about the contract Dave signed with him?" Anna asked. "Is he the one threatening her?"

"He said Sandy asked him to meet her."

"He could be lying," she said.

"I'll do some checking." He would start by finding out where George Anton had been when Dave Weiss died.

Someone whistled and Anna put a hand on Lucas's arm. "I have to go," she said. "It was good to see you."

"It was good to see—" But she was already gone, back to the group of volunteers who were loading up equipment and preparing to leave. Lucas strung tape to close off the pullout where the emergency vehicles had parked, to keep the curious from stopping to look. He had worked one wreck where, though the driver of the vehicle escaped with only minor injuries, a would-be good Samaritan who'd decided to check out the wreck had fallen and died.

Then he headed back to the sheriff's office, intent on finding out as much as he could about George Anton.

ANNA CHANGED CLOTHES at Search and Rescue headquarters, back into the wool skirt, hand-knit sweater,
tights and boots that were her winter work uniform.
She had intended to drive straight to the shop, but
instead turned onto the side street that led to Weiss
Bakery.

A single car was parked in the gravel lot in front
of the white-brick structure. A former meat processing plant, the building sat by itself at the end of a
street on the edge of town, surrounded by empty pas-
ture. A sign at the end of the street and another on
the building itself directed customers to the bakery.
Dave's talent for producing delicious and beautiful
desserts had attracted customers who were willing
to go a little out of their way to shop there, though
today the place looked almost empty.

Anna pushed open the door and inhaled the familiar aromas of sugar and vanilla. The front room
was empty, the glass bakery case about half full of
various pastries, cookies and cupcakes. Anna looked
around. "Hello?" she called.

A moment later, Sandy emerged from a back room,
a twenty-five-pound bag of flour under each arm.
The frown lines on her forehead deepened when she
recognized Anna. "What are you doing here?" she
asked. She deposited the bags of flour on a wooden
table at the far end of the counter and brushed a white
smudge from the side of her blue sweatshirt.

"I wanted to see how you were doing." Anna moved
to the bakery case.

"I'm fine." Sandy picked up a white bar towel and

began wiping down the glass case at the end of the counter.

"I just came from a search and rescue call," Anna said. "An Escalade went off the road on Dakota Ridge. The driver was George Anton."

Sandy went still. "Is he dead?" she asked.

"No. Just a bump on the head. He's on his way now to the hospital to be checked out. The woman with him, Shaylin Brown, wasn't so lucky. She had a lot of cuts from glass, and maybe a broken arm. She was in a lot of pain." She watched Sandy carefully, trying to read her reaction, but she only blinked a couple of times then went back to wiping down the glass.

"Mr. Anton said he had just come from a meeting with you," Anna said.

"So what if he was?" Sandy stopped wiping and glared at Anna. "Maybe you think I should be collapsed in a heap, mourning my husband, but I don't have that luxury. I have a business to take care of."

Anna drew back, stung. "I don't think that at all," she said. "I'm not judging you, Sandy. Not at all. I've always admired how strong and practical you are. And I know there is no one right way to mourn."

Sandy tossed the rag into a white plastic bucket behind her. "Sorry. I've just had my fill of people telling me how 'shocked' they are that I'm selling the house, or they can't believe I didn't close the bakery for a week 'out of respect for Dave.' Until they're paying my bills, they need to shut up." She bit her lip and looked away, blinking rapidly.

Any other person, Anna might have reached out to offer a literal shoulder to cry on, but she doubted Sandy would appreciate the gesture. "Maybe you could negotiate with your creditors," she said. "I'm sure the local bank would understand you need more time…"

"George Anton is our creditor," Sandy said. "He's the one who loaned us the money to expand. Low interest, good terms. He promised to send enough business our way, we would be more than able to pay, but that didn't happen."

"Is that even legal?" Anna asked.

"Don't look at me like I'm a fool," Sandy snapped. "I never should have told you."

Anna took a step back. "I'm sure you'll deal with things the way that's best for you," she said.

"I'll deal with them all right."

Silence stretched between them. Anna searched for something to say that wouldn't make Sandy even angrier. "Have you had any more threatening calls or letters?" she asked.

Sandy shook her head. "Maybe it was just a prankster," she said. "Apparently, death can bring out sickos who like to prey on the families left behind. Or so I've read."

"If there's anything I can do to help, please tell me," Anna said.

"Why do you want to help me?" Sandy challenged, defensive once more.

"I know what's it's like to be in your shoes," Anna

said. Widowed young, with no family close. Alone in the worst way.

"I doubt that," Sandy said.

The door opened and a couple entered, talking loudly about their dinner party plans. Anna debated waiting until they'd made their purchases and left and trying to resume her conversation with Sandy, but decided against it. She wasn't doing anything but upsetting the poor woman, who either couldn't—or didn't want to—tell her any more about the threats or George Anton or anything relating to Dave's death.

Anna knew she had no "right" to such information. But finding Dave's body had shaken her more than her other body recoveries. Dave had been Jonas's friend, and her friend, too. How could she—or Sandy—lay him to rest without knowing what had really happened to him?

"Goodbye," she said. Though Sandy, who had already turned to wait on her customers, didn't acknowledge her words. She returned to her car and drove to Yarn and More, still unsettled by Sandy's prickly attitude. She needed to lose herself for a while in the soothing colors and textures of yarn.

"How did it go?" Gemma asked when Anna settled beside her at the worktable.

It took a moment before Anna realized her friend was referring to the rescue. "It went well. Some injuries, but both driver and passenger should recover."

"That's great," Gemma said. She leaned closer, studying Anna's face. "But you look upset. Did something else happen?"

Anna picked up the half-finished scarf from the workbag beside her chair and began to knit. "I stopped by the bakery to see Sandy."

Gemma sat back. "Did she say something to upset you?"

"What makes you think that?"

"Because I know Sandy. She's always gone out of her way to be rude to you."

Anna almost dropped a stitch, she was so startled. She pushed the knitting away. "Sandy isn't rude, she's just…brusque."

"She was rude to you," Gemma said. "Frankly, I think she's always been jealous."

"Why would she be jealous?" Anna asked. "There wasn't anything in my life she wanted."

"Except that people like you. People put up with Sandy because of Dave. And she pulls her own weight at the fire department, I'll give you that. Her fellow volunteers respect her, but I don't think many of them really like her. She doesn't have the easy way with people you have."

"I'm sure you're wrong about that," Anna said. "Sandy has lots of friends, not just with the fire department. There are the people she bikes with, and climbers."

"They were Dave's friends first," Gemma noted. She began straightening items on the table, stacking pattern books and corralling yarn into a basket. "What did she say to upset you?"

"I told her to tell me if there was anything I could do to help her and she all but accused me of having an ulterior motive. I tried to tell her I understood what she was going through and she took it all wrong."

"I don't know why you bother," Gemma said. "If she doesn't want your help, why keep offering?"

"Because I know what it's like to lose the man you loved so young," Anna said. "I remember how much I appreciated everyone who came to help me, and I want to pass that on to Sandy. It doesn't take away the loss, but it does help." She picked up the scarf again but didn't resume working on it. She held the project in her lap, stroking the soft yarn and admiring the interplay of colors. "I'm sure I was upset and said things to people I shouldn't have. Grief exposes every nerve. People were willing to overlook that for me, so I'm trying to do the same for Sandy."

Gemma reached over and squeezed Anna's wrist. "I can't imagine you ever said anything terrible to anyone, but if you did, it's easier to forgive a nice, likeable person."

"I always thought the challenge of forgiveness was supposed to be that it's hard." She slipped the tip of the needle beneath the first stitch and wrapped the yarn. "Anyway, I'm trying to give Sandy the space she seems to want, but also be there if she needs anything. Dave wouldn't want her to have to handle everything by herself, and he was dear to me, and to Jonas."

"That just proves you're a better person than I am." Gemma checked her watch then bounced to her feet. "I have to go. I promised Terry I'd meet him for lunch." She grabbed up her purse and coat, and hurried out the door.

Anna continued knitting, her mind still racing as she completed each stitch. She wanted to call Justin, but he would tell her she was interfering with things that didn't concern her. He would probably be angry. He might even accuse her of trying to upset him on purpose.

He wouldn't be entirely wrong. But she had long since stopped caring what he thought of her. She set the scarf aside and pulled out her phone. Justin answered with his usual brusqueness. "Two calls in one week, Anna. What is going on?"

"Shaylin Brown was injured in a car accident this afternoon," she said. "I thought you'd want to know."

Silence, though she thought she heard him get up and close the door. He was probably in his office at the restaurant. "How do you know anything about Shaylin?" he asked.

"Eagle Mountain Search and Rescue responded to the call," she said. "Shaylin was with George Anton. Apparently, she works for him now."

"I know that. What happened?"

"His car hit a patch of ice and went off the road at Dakota Ridge. They were lucky they weren't killed."

"Why did you call to tell me this?"

"I thought you might want to know."

"Shaylin and I aren't involved anymore. That was a mistake I will pay for for the rest of my life, and I don't appreciate you bringing it up."

"I just thought you might want to know she was hurt. She's in the hospital in Junction."

"I'm sorry to hear that, but it's not my concern."

"What do you know about George Anton?" she asked.

"I already told you. He supplies food to restaurants. He supplies my restaurant."

"But what else do you know about him?" Was he the type who would threaten a customer like Sandy? Could he have killed Dave?

"I don't have to know the life story of everyone I do business with," Justin said. "We came to an agreement that benefits both of us and that's all we have to know. Why are you even asking these questions?"

"Because someone has been threatening Sandy Weiss, Dave's widow," she said. "I wondered if it might be George."

"Why would George threaten Sandy?" Justin asked.

"She owes him money."

He laughed. "A lot of people owe me money and I don't threaten them. It's not how most businesses operate."

She decided to shift the conversation. Maybe she could throw him off guard. "Why did you call the sheriff's department about me?"

"I don't think it's safe or smart to meddle in a police investigation," he said, seemingly unmoved.

"I don't need you to look after me, Justin."

"Apparently, you do, if you're going to go around playing amateur detective. You're Jonas's widow and I feel an obligation to him."

"He's been gone two years and this is the first time you've showed any concern for me," she said.

"This is the first time I've become aware that you're behaving so foolishly."

She took a deep breath and forced herself to count to ten. Justin was saying this to make her angry and to deflect attention from him and his motives. She had seen him do it before, or attempt to do it. Jonas had seldom fallen for his brother's manipulation.

"I don't think I'm being foolish, but I am trying to help a friend," she said. "And I thought you might want to know about Shaylin. Even if you aren't seeing her now, you were close once."

"Do me a favor and don't make any assumptions about me and my feelings." He ended the call before she could say anything.

She pocketed her phone. That went about as well as she had expected. Justin wasn't her favorite person, but his restaurant had a good reputation and Jonas had always said his brother was one of the savviest business people he knew. Justin stayed out of debt and made money.

He wouldn't have signed a contract with George Anton unless he thought it was a way to make more money, so how had Dave ended up in debt to Anton? And not just a little debt. Sandy made the situation sound dire, if she was having to sell her house and the bakery building to make the payments.

The list of questions she wished she could learn the answers to grew longer every day. The bell over the door rang and she looked up, a smile on her face, determined to focus on the things she did know, including how to help her customers find just the items they needed. If only she had someone to help her do the same.

ON MONDAY MORNING, one week after Dave Weiss's body had been found, the sheriff convened a meeting to review the case. "The medical examiner has ruled the cause of death was a broken neck, but he's unable to determine whether this was due to suicide or murder," Travis said. "I want us to review what we know and see if we can draw any conclusions."

"Those dog tranquilizers in his system seem suspicious," Sergeant Gage Walker, the sheriff's brother, said.

"And why that location?" Wes Landry asked. "If Dave was intent on hanging himself, there are a lot of places it would be easier to do it."

"Maybe the location had some significance to him we don't know about yet," Shane Ellis interjected.

"Or maybe he didn't want his body found easily," Dwight Prentice said. "Even with his truck there, we might not have found him for days or weeks if not for Anna Trent and her search dog."

"Anna knew Dave and she seemed surprised he would take his own life," Lucas said. He wondered how much her doubts had influenced him. If he hadn't been so focused on her and her emotions, would he have automatically taken the scene at face value—a man in despair who had decided to end his life?

"The branch the rope was tied off on was pretty high up in that tree," Travis noted. "Not an impossible climb, but a difficult one."

"He wanted to make sure the drop was far enough for a quick end," Gage said.

"Or his killer wanted that," Lucas said. "And there are those impressions in the ground beneath his body. They sure look like a ladder to me."

"So his killer not only gets Dave back to that remote location, he hauls a ladder back there?" Shane shook his head.

"Dave wasn't a little man," Gage said. "Even doped up, he would probably try to fight. I don't see how anyone could get him up that ladder."

"Order him up at gunpoint," Dwight suggested.

"Or threaten his family," Wes said. "Promise to kill his wife if he didn't cooperate."

"Sandy doesn't think it's suicide," Lucas said.

"Families often are in denial," Wes observed. "That's understandable."

"She thought at first that he had killed himself," Lucas said. "But those threatening phone calls and the note made her think differently."

"We weren't able to trace the calls or find anything significant about the note," Gage said. "It was on common notebook paper and the letters were cut from a magazine, but we can't get more specific than that. The message was vague and threatening, but nonspecific."

"So maybe just a prank," Dwight proposed. "Someone with a sick sense of humor."

"We need to take a closer look at George Anton," Travis said. "Sandy says the contract Dave signed with him was the source of their financial trouble."

"She confirmed she met with Anton yesterday afternoon," Lucas said. He had spoken briefly with Sandy after the accident. Apparently, Anna had already broken the news of the rescue, shortly before Lucas called. "Anton was coming from that meeting when he was injured in that accident up on Dakota Ridge."

"What about the woman who was with Anton?" Gage asked. "What was her role in this?"

"Anton said she worked for him and was along to put Sandy at ease," Lucas told him. He didn't bother mentioning Shaylin Brown's former relationship with Anna's brother-in-law. It was interesting, but he didn't see that it had any bearing on the case.

"That doesn't sound threatening," Dwight said.

"I ran Anton's name and didn't come up with anything," Lucas said. "No criminal record, and his only online profiles are in relation to his business, Anton's Finest. I didn't find a motive for him to threaten Sandy or want to harm Dave. With Dave gone, his chances of getting money he's owed from commissions, or the desserts Dave contracted to supply, go down."

"Any other ideas where the threats came from?" Gage asked.

Lucas shook his head. "Sandy says no. And she doesn't know of any similar threats Dave might have received before he died."

"We need to go through Dave's belongings and

his business records," Travis said. "Maybe we'll find something there."

"I'm headed to the bakery to do that this morning," Lucas advised. "It would help if we could find Dave's phone. It's missing, and Anna says he might have used it instead of a laptop or tablet. I've requested his phone records but I'm not having any luck tracing the phone's location."

"For now, the case stays open," Travis said.

When the meeting was over, Lucas drove to the bakery. The business sat at the end of a dead-end street on the very edge of town, surrounded by empty fields. A small corral behind the white-brick structure was empty, and a large roll-down door on one side of the building had a sturdy padlock on it.

Sandy was on the phone when Lucas stepped inside. "What do you want it to say on the top of the cake?" she asked her caller, and made a note on the clipboard in front of her. "What color would you like the lettering?"

While he waited for her to finish the call, Lucas looked around the bakery. There were posters advertising wedding cakes and holiday pies, and a row of photographs in black plastic frames: Dave and Sandy in bunker gear. Sandy on a mountain bike on a trail. Dave with a massive lake trout. An active life spent outdoors.

"Have you found out anything, Deputy?"

He turned back to Sandy. She stood behind the front counter, her hands in the pockets of a blue apron. "Not yet," he said. "I need to look through Dave's office and the bakery's computer."

"I've already looked," she said. "You're not going to find anything."

He had dealt with this kind of reluctance before. No one wanted a stranger, much less a police officer, going through their personal records. "I might see something you didn't," he said. "And anything I find is held in confidence, unless it's evidence we need to use at a trial."

She pursed her lips. "It just seems so...intrusive."

It was intrusive. In the course of investigations, he had read personal love letters, people's attempts at bad fiction, and accessed secret porn accounts. He hadn't lingered over any of those, as they hadn't pertained to the cases he'd been involved in at the time. But just knowing he was going to see such highly personal things made most people uncomfortable. "It's important to gather as much information as possible to find out what happened to your husband," he said. "And to track down who threatened you."

"I haven't heard anything else," she said. "I think it was just a sick joke."

"I still need to look through Dave's things."

"Aren't you supposed to have a warrant or something?"

Now he wondered just what she thought he would find. "I could get one, but it will be faster if you agree to let me search. The sooner we gather information, the better."

She chewed her lower lip. "All right. But I don't

think you're going to find anything. Dave kept everything personal on his phone."

She led the way through the door behind the bakery counter, into a surprisingly spartan office. The desktop was clear of everything except a page-a-day calendar stuck on the day before Dave had died. The cinder block walls were bare and the single window high in the wall looked out onto an alley. "This seems like a remote location for a bakery," he said. "There aren't any other businesses around."

"This building used to be a meat processor," Sandy said. "They kept cows in the corral out there until slaughter. You don't really want that kind of thing right downtown. We bought it because it was cheap. We figured the baked goods we made were good enough people would drive out here, and we were right."

"I heard your specialty is something called a Surprise Cake," he said.

"That's right. You can choose one of our surprise fillings or we'll include your own. We've put engagement rings, birthday gifts, party favors—all kinds of things inside. The hollow to hold the surprise is made after the cake is baked, so you can put anything in there. We once put a positive pregnancy test in a cupcake." She shrugged. "If the customer wants it, we'll put it in there."

"I'd better get started," he said.

"Suit yourself."

She left him alone. He started with the desk. Deep drawers on either side of the desk held files full of the forms people filled out to order cakes or pastries. There were receipts for supplies, licensing paperwork, health department paperwork, and records of donations the bakery had made to local softball teams and other charities.

After less than thirty minutes, Lucas had seen everything there was to see in the space. He moved to the doorway and spoke to Sandy, who was marking down the price on a tray of bear claws. "Where are the financial records?" he asked. "The day-to-day accounts, I mean."

"Our CPA keeps track of all that," she said, not looking up from her work.

"Don't you have computer records here?"

"Dave didn't like computers."

How did anyone operate a business in this day and age without computerized records? "What about an old-fashioned ledger?"

She shook her head. "Our CPA takes care of everything."

"Then I'll need to talk to your CPA."

"I'll have to talk to him about that. He's probably going to want to see something more official."

If he was any good at his job, he would, Lucas thought. "Where is the contract Dave signed with George Anton?" he asked.

She glanced over her shoulder at him. "You didn't find it?"

"No."

She slid the tray of pastries into the glass case, stripped off her gloves, dropped them in the trash

can, then followed him into the office. She opened
one of the desk drawers. "It should be in here," she
said, and riffled through the files. She closed that
drawer and turned to the others. At last, she looked
up at him. "It should be right here, but it's not."

"Was it there when you searched the office?"

"I didn't notice. I was just looking for anything
out of place."

He frowned. He hadn't found any threatening
notes, and he hadn't found the contract with Anton.
Nothing that pertained to the case. Nothing to indicate Dave was thinking about suicide, either.

"I'd like to see the house. Maybe he kept some
things there you didn't know about."

She thrust her hands back into the pockets of
her apron. "You'll have to wait until I close at five-
thirty."

"You can give me a house key."

She took a step back. "I don't want you nosing
around when I'm not there."

He could have pressed, but didn't. "Did you and
Dave ever have a dog?" he asked.

"No."

"What about before you married? Did you have
a dog? Did Dave?"

"No. I mean, I think he might have had a dog or
two when he was a little kid, but not as an adult. We
had a cat for a few years, but after he ran off, we decided pets tied us down too much. Why are you asking about a dog?"

"The medical examiner found that Dave had a

sedative in his system when he died. It's a drug commonly used to control seizures in dogs."

She stared. "That's the strangest thing anyone's ever told me. You're saying Dave took dog tranquilizers?"

"It's a human medication that is used in dogs, too. But the vet here doesn't prescribe it." The Eagle Mountain vet had explained he preferred different medications that didn't have the side effects of phenobarbital.

"Maybe your lab got something wrong," Sandy said.

He doubted it, but wasn't going to debate her.

"What's going on with you and Anna?" Sandy asked.

Her question caught him off guard, which may have been why she'd asked it.

"We had dinner together," he said. It wasn't any of her business, but it wasn't a secret, either.

"You know she's a widow. Practically a newlywed still when her husband died."

"I know." Did she think the fact that Anna had been married before would put him off?

"I'm a practical person. Sad as I am about losing Dave, I know life goes on. I have to move forward and make the best of things. Anna isn't like that. She idolized Jonas. No other man is ever going to measure up."

He stiffened. "I'm not looking to 'measure up' to anyone. We just had dinner."

She shrugged. "Suit yourself." The phone rang.

"I have to go." She pushed past him into the office again, and shut the door behind her.

He stared after her, half a dozen different retorts stalled in his head. But ahead of all the snappy comebacks he might have made was the question Sandy's words had raised in his mind. Was Anna still in love with her dead husband? Should he walk away before he made a mistake and started thinking past dinner?

Death changed so much. It was awful in the moment, and awful for months or years afterward, as those left behind lived with the reality of unrealized hopes and regrets for all they would never say or do. People learned to live with that, and to be hopeful and happy again, but they couldn't live as if death hadn't changed them. Those who knew them best could see the scars. He saw them in himself, and he recognized them in Anna. That shared suffering made him feel close to her, but he wasn't so sure it was a good basis for a relationship.

Not that he wanted a relationship. It was just… good to be with someone who knew his story. Anna wouldn't expect too much from him.

Jenny had expected too much from him. His greatest regret was that he hadn't been able to give her what she'd expected, much less what she'd deserved.

At five-twenty, Lucas left the sheriff's department and drove to the Weisses' house. The red For Sale sign stood out against the accumulated snow on the front lawn. The house already looked empty, with no furniture on the porch, no car in the drive. He parked at the curb and five minutes later Sandy pulled into the drive. She got out of her car and headed to the front door without acknowledging him. "You're wasting your time," she said as he came up behind her while she was unlocking the door. "There's nothing here that will help you figure out what happened to Dave."

"You never know," he said and followed her inside.

The first thing he noticed was how empty the house felt. The living room and the dining room next to it were almost devoid of furniture, only a single upholstered chair and a lamp sitting in the middle of an expanse of dull beige carpet. "There's no point in keeping things if I'm going to be moving," Sandy said.

He followed her farther into the house, past the door to the kitchen, down a hallway to a room with a queen-sized bed, a small table with a lamp and a row of cardboard boxes along one wall. She pointed to a closet. "That was Dave's, but I've already given away most of his things."

He opened his mouth to ask why she had done that, but she cut him off. "I thought he killed himself. Seeing his things was too painful, so I bagged everything up and took it to the humane society thrift store in Junction."

He nodded. He had been tempted to do the same with everything that had belonged to Jenny after she'd died. Instead, he had asked her sister to take everything.

He opened the closet door and looked at the empty shelves and hangers. A single shirt button rested on the edge of one shelf, and a worn belt hung from a nail at the very back. He shook his head and closed the door behind him.

Sandy had left the room, so he moved to her closet. In contrast to Dave's, her space was crammed with clothing—shirts, pants, a few skirts and dresses and winter coats, as well as at least twenty pairs of boots and shoes, various cycling and workout gear, a hamper of dirty laundry. He sighed and began going through everything.

He found several shirts that might have belonged to Dave, but there was nothing in the pockets. He moved on to the dresser, which also yielded nothing of Dave's and also nothing that revealed any insights into Sandy. She wore little jewelry, preferred casual clothing and practical footwear, and if she had displayed any personal photos in the bedroom, she must have packed them away.

He found her in the kitchen, standing at the counter, drinking coffee from a mug that advertised a local bank. "Did you ask your CPA about those financial records?" he asked.

"Not yet." She sipped the coffee and fixed him with a cold stare. Not exactly hostile. Annoyed, maybe.

"Did Dave keep any financial or business records here?"

"No," she said.

"Did he have a home office?"

"He had a desk. But I already gave that away, too."

"What did you do with the contents of the desk?" he asked.

"I burned it all." She smiled, as if pleased to frustrate him with this news. "I looked through it all before I lit the match," she added. "There was nothing there. No personal diary, no suicide note, no plans for his demise."

"What about threats? Did you find anything like that?"

"Nothing."

He looked around the kitchen. Two cabinet doors stood open, showing the insides were empty. Three more cardboard boxes sat on the counter, one open to reveal packed dishes. He was wasting his time here. "Where's your bathroom?" he asked.

"Down the hall, next to the bedroom," she said. "There's only the one."

In the bathroom, he did a quick check of the medicine cabinet and the shelves beneath the sink. He found an assortment of over-the-counter remedies and some expired prescription allergy medication for Sandy. No phenobarbital. No sleeping pills or anti-anxiety medications or anything that might indicate Dave or Sandy had been dealing with extra stress.

Sandy appeared in the doorway. "Are you done yet?" she asked.

He looked up from examining the spare towels under the sink. "I want to see the garage," he said.

She led him out the back door to a detached, single-car garage behind the house. It, too, had been stripped bare. Not a single old paint can rested on the shelves between the studs of the walls, and only an oil stain on the concrete floor gave evidence that the building had ever been used at all. "A guy from Delta made me a good offer on everything that was in there," Sandy said. "He hauled it all off yesterday."

Lucas shook his head. Maybe he would have found something significant if he had gotten here before Sandy had donated or burned all of Dave's things. But he was too late now.

He left and sat in his cruiser for a moment, debating whether he should return to the office and go through the case files one more time. His phone rang and his spirits lifted when he saw Anna's name on the screen.

"Hello," he answered. "How are you?"

"Not so good right now."

The shake in her voice made him sit up straighter. "What's wrong?"

"I just got home from work. There's a note on my front door. It says…" Her voice faltered and he heard her inhale shakily. "It says if I'm not careful, I'll be the next person to die!"

Chapter Nine

Anna sat in her porch swing, coat pulled tightly around her against the cold, and waited for Lucas to arrive. Jacquie curled against her, her head in Anna's lap. She threaded her fingers through Jacquie's curls and watched the street, resolutely averting her eyes from the single sheet of lined paper tacked to her front door. But she didn't have to see it to remember what it looked like or what it said: Mind your own business or you will be the next to die.

The words were melodramatic, bad B-movie dialogue. But they were also terrifying.

A black-and-white sheriff's department SUV turned onto her street and she stood and walked to the edge of the porch. Jacquie jumped up and came to sit beside her. They waited while Lucas parked and strode up the walk toward them. "Are you all right?" he asked, searching her face.

"I'm fine." She turned toward the door. "It's just a piece of paper, but who would do something like this?"

She followed him to the door. He studied the note a moment then took out his phone and photographed it from several angles. Then he took a large, clear, plastic envelope from his jacket, along with a pair of nitrile gloves. He put on the gloves, then carefully pried loose the thumbtack holding the note in place and slid both tack and note into the envelope. He completed a label on the front and tucked the whole thing back into his jacket, along with the gloves. "What time did you find it?" he asked.

"I close the shop at six and I drove straight home, so about ten after six," she said.

"Did you touch it?"

She shook her head. "No. I read the words. Then I read them again. I looked around—I don't know why. It's not as if whoever did this would stand around waiting for my reaction. And Jacquie didn't act upset, as if she sensed a stranger nearby. Then I sat in the swing and called you." She had sat because her legs wouldn't support her, and she had called him because she knew she would feel stronger and safer if he were with her, instead of whatever deputy might be on duty.

"What time did you leave the house this morning?"

"A quarter to ten. I usually try to be at the shop by nine, so I have an hour to work before we open, but I didn't sleep well last night, so got a late start." She had tossed and turned much of the night, her emotions in turmoil.

"I want to talk to your neighbors and see if any of them noticed anyone near your house today." He touched her shoulder. "Will you be all right here while I do that?"

"Of course." She glanced down at Jacquie, who sat beside her, leaning heavily against her leg. "And I have Jacquie." The poodle didn't have an ounce of meanness in her, but she could bark loudly, and her large size intimidated some people.

He left and crossed the street. Anna shivered and decided it was ridiculous for her to stay out here in the cold. She unlocked the front door and went in, letting the dog go first. If a stranger did lurk inside, Jacquie would find him or her.

But the house was empty. Jacquie trotted to her water bowl and drank loudly while Anna hung up her coat and then followed her into the kitchen. She put on the kettle and looked out the kitchen window, hoping to glimpse Lucas on his way to or from a neighbor's house, but the street was empty.

A knock on the door announced his return just as the teakettle began to whistle. She shut off the stove then hurried to open the door. "A woman across the street saw a delivery person here just after noon," he said. "Someone in a brown shirt and pants, a ball cap, with short hair. She said 'he' but admitted it could have been a woman. The person went up to all the houses on this side of the street. I double-checked, and none of them received any deliveries today."

"Come into the kitchen," she said.

He followed her, shedding his coat once there and draping it over the back of one of the chairs around the table. "I'm making tea," she said. "Do you want some? Or cocoa?"

"No thanks." He pulled out a chair and sat. "Can

you think of anything that might have set someone off?" he asked. "Something that would have triggered that person to post this note? Something that made them feel threatened?"

She sat across from him. "No! It's just bizarre. I'm not a threat to anyone."

"Tell me everything you did the last three days," he said. "Everyone you talked to."

"There was the search and rescue call Saturday—you know about that. When that was done, I stopped by the bakery."

"Why did you do that?"

"I wanted to see how Sandy was doing. And I wanted to find out more about George Anton and Sandy's meeting with him." She flushed. "I know it's none of my business, but I want to know."

"What did she tell you?"

"Not much," she admitted. "She ranted a little about how she was angry at people for judging her for running the bakery and putting it and the house up for sale instead of collapsing in a grief-stricken heap. I told her about Anton's accident, but once I assured her he wasn't dead, she lost interest. She really didn't tell me much about the meeting, only that they had had one." She stirred her tea. "I would make a terrible detective. I don't know how to be subtle when questioning people."

"Did Sandy seem angry with you?"

"No. She was how she always is with me—not hostile, but not terribly friendly. The two of us rub each other the wrong way. She makes me feel inadequate and awkward, and she seems to think I'm silently judging her. I actually admire her a great deal, but she never believes me when I say so."

"All right. Anybody else?"

"There was Gemma and customers at the shop, of course, but none of them are going to threaten to kill me." She sipped her tea, choosing her words. "I talked to one more person Saturday. And he's not my biggest fan, either." She forced herself to meet Lucas's steady gaze. "I called Justin. I wanted to gauge his reaction when I told him about Shaylin Brown. That's probably petty of me, and he called me on it, which I deserved."

"What else did he have to say?"

"Just that George Anton offered a good deal to suppliers and restaurants." She gripped her teacup more tightly as a new thought swept over her. "Do you think Justin could have told George I was asking about him? If he's the one who made those threats to Sandy, maybe he decided to do the same to me."

"We haven't found any evidence linking George Anton to those threats," he said. "We haven't found evidence linking anyone to them." He pulled out his phone. "Let me check something right quick."

He waited for a moment then identified himself to the person on the other end of the line. "Can you tell me when George Anton was released from treatment? He was transported to the hospital from Rayford County yesterday morning."

Another pause then he said, "What about the woman who was with him? Shaylin Brown?"

He made some notes, said thank-you, and ended

the call. "George Anton was treated and released yesterday afternoon," he said. "Shaylin Brown was discharged at two this afternoon. So she couldn't have been the person who left this note, but Anton could have been."

"If he is the one sending these threats, that must mean he has something to hide," she said. "Something to protect." She shuddered. How far would he go to hide or protect whatever that was?

"I'll talk to him, see if he has an alibi," Lucas said. "And we'll compare this note to the one Sandy gave us."

"It looked the same," she said. "They both might have been torn from the same notebook."

"We'll double-check to be sure, but they look the same to me, too. What about the rest of the weekend and today?" he asked. "Who did you see or talk to those days?"

"Sunday, I cleaned house and watched TV and knitted. I didn't see or talk to anyone. Today, I worked at the shop. I talked to Gemma and customers, but nothing upsetting or unusual. Mostly, we talked about yarn and knitting."

He nodded and made notes on a small pad he'd pulled from his pocket. She sat up straighter. Now that the first shock of that note had worn off, she was growing angrier. "Have you found out anything else about Dave's death?" she asked.

"I searched his office today, but there was nothing," Lucas said. "No sign that he was either being threatened or that he was contemplating suicide. But not everyone writes that sort of thing down."

She took another sip of tea, which had grown cold and bitter. She pushed the mug aside. "Something struck me when I was talking to Justin," she said. "He was talking about how the arrangement with George Anton was a good deal for both of them. Justin has run a successful restaurant for almost fifteen years. He's a good businessman. He wouldn't make a deal that didn't benefit him and make him money. So how did Dave, who was also in a contract with Anton, end up with so much debt? He wasn't as wily as Justin, but he had never had financial trouble as long as I've known him."

"Maybe things weren't as advantageous on the supplier's side," Lucas said. "Or maybe the debt isn't due to the contract with Anton, but with how far he extended himself with loans for the new cooler and more help and supplies."

"But all those loans were with Anton, too."

"They were? How did I miss that?"

"Sandy let it slip then acted like she wished she hadn't told me. Apparently, Anton agreed to loan them the money to expand in order to supply more desserts for the restaurants that were also his clients. Sandy said he offered a low interest rate and promised to give them sufficient business to enable them to pay on the loan and take a small profit, but it didn't work that way."

"I wonder how many other people Anton has with similar agreements," Lucas said.

"Is what he's doing illegal?"

"I don't think so, but that's not my area of expertise. I'll ask my colleagues in Junction if they know anything." He slid back his chair. "How are you feeling now?"

"Steadier." She smiled. "That note is so ridiculous, it's hard to be afraid now that I've had time to think about it. It's unsettling, yes, but also too over-the-top. If you really intended to kill someone, would you give them so much warning?"

"Maybe the aim isn't murder, but silence," Lucas said.

"Then it would help if they told me what I'm supposed to be silent about."

"Will you be okay here alone?" he asked. "I'll ask the deputy on duty tonight to drive by a few times to check on things. Or you could come to my house. I have a decent guest room."

Her heart beat a little faster at the thought of spending the night at his house—though not necessarily in the guest room. She stood, also. "I'll be fine alone," she said. "Though, why don't you stay for dinner? Do you really want to go home and eat alone? I know I don't."

He smiled. "I'd like that."

She pulled out chicken and vegetables to make a pasta dish. "You can chop the peppers while I peel carrots," she said and handed him several bags of produce from the refrigerator.

When she closed the refrigerator, he paused to study the pictures there. He nodded to the photo of her and Jonas, with Sandy and Dave, atop Dakota Ridge. "Is that your husband?"

"Yes."

"You look happy together. I imagine you loved him very much."

"Yes. I always will. I'm sure it's the same with you and your girlfriend."

He met her gaze briefly, something troubled there, then looked away. "Yes." He turned and set the produce on the counter then pulled a knife from the block. "How do you want these peppers sliced?"

She was determined to overcome this sudden awkwardness. They ought to be able to talk about their exes without feeling like this. "How did you and Jenny meet?" she asked.

He didn't look up from his chopping. "She worked at the tax office, just down the hall from the police department where I did a stint as a civilian volunteer, while I was waiting to get into the academy."

"A cousin introduced me to Jonas," she said. "We hit it off right away."

"Jenny refused to go out with me for three weeks," he said. "She said she never wanted to be involved with a cop."

"What changed her mind?"

He finally looked up, his wicked grin making her laugh. "My devastating charm, of course." He held up the cutting board. "Do these look okay?"

"They're great. Now, would you start a pot of water boiling for the pasta?" She paused before returning to their conversation. "What drew you to police work?" she asked as he filled a pot with water.

"It sounds corny to say I wanted to make a difference, but it's true. And I thought I had a good temperament for it. I don't mind working alone, and I don't have trouble talking to people. Every day is different. A lot of the job is boring, but some of it is intensely interesting. It's not for everyone, but I like it."

As the topic shifted to their backgrounds and interests, the mood grew more relaxed. This was more like a first date than the dinner they had had the other night, she thought. Then, they had talked mostly about Dave's death. Now, they were getting to know each other, and she liked what she was finding out.

"This looks delicious," he said later when they sat down to dinner. "Thanks for inviting me to stay."

"You're good company," she said.

"So are you." Their eyes met and she felt a tingle down to her toes. The sensation surprised her. It made her a little nervous. But it also made her hopeful. Not all of her had died with Jonas.

He insisted on helping clean the dishes and she considered asking him to stay a little longer, for coffee or a glass of wine. Would she ask him to stay the night? *Too soon*, she thought, but she enjoyed contemplating the idea. It didn't make her nearly as nervous as she would have thought such a big step would. Maybe that was because at least part of her was ready to move on into a future without Jonas. Yes, he had been gone two years, but he was still such a huge, important part of her life. Maybe she was working toward letting him go, so they could both rest in peace.

"I'd better go," Lucas said, wiping his hand on a dish towel. "If you're sure you'll be okay on your own?"

Here was her chance to ask him to stay but, clearly, he needed to leave. "I'll be fine," she said.

She waited while he shrugged into his coat and followed him to the door. Jacquie watched from her place on the end of the sofa. "Thanks for dinner," he said.

"I had a nice time," she said. She put a hand on his arm. "We'll have to do it again sometime." Her eyes met his, trying to tell him how attracted she was to him. She shifted her gaze to his lips and leaned a little closer, sure he would take the hint and kiss her good night, and maybe continue what they had started the other night before Sandy had interrupted them.

"I'll look around outside before I leave," he said then opened the door and was gone.

She waited by the window, watching as he switched on a flashlight and circled the house. When he reached the front once more, he gave her a thumbs-up gesture and strode to his SUV. She hugged her arms across her stomach and stalked back to the sofa. So much for her own "devastating charm." Lucas Malone was apparently immune.

Chapter Ten

Tuesday morning, Anna was marking down yarn for the sale bin when Sandy called her. "Can we get together for drinks after work?" Sandy asked.

"Uh, sure." Sandy had never asked Anna to any activity that didn't include Dave and Jonas, too. Now that they were both widowed, were Anna's efforts to be Sandy's friend paying off? "I'd love to."

"Meet me at Mo's at six fifteen." Not waiting for confirmation, she ended the call.

"Is something wrong?" Gemma dumped an armload of yarn onto the worktable. "You look upset."

"No, nothing's wrong." She picked up the pricing gun again. "Sandy Weiss invited me for drinks at Mo's tonight."

"You don't look too happy about it," Gemma said.

"No, I'm happy. It was just…unexpected." She picked up a skein of cashmere. This orange shade had been a slow seller and she needed to clear it out to make room for new stock. "I'm thinking of doing a display of one-skein projects. What do you think?"

"It's a good way of encouraging people to buy

some of the pricier yarn," Gemma said. "One skein doesn't make such a dent in the budget. Does Sandy knit or crochet?"

"I don't think so." Sandy had never showed interest in Anna's own hand-knit items, and she had once declared she didn't see the point of crafts of any kind.

"Maybe you can convert her. It's a great stress reliever."

Sandy probably relieved her stress by trail running or lifting heavy weights. Nothing wrong with that, of course, though Anna preferred yoga and knitting. She smiled at the thought that she and Sandy were truly opposites when it came to almost everything. But that didn't mean they couldn't be better friends.

A trio of customers entered—two women who were clearly together, and Kyle Saddler, who caught the door as it started to close behind them.

"Hello, Anna," he said, zeroing in on her.

"Hello, Kyle," she said. "How did your niece like her birthday gift?"

His expression clouded for a moment then cleared. "Oh, my niece. She liked it a lot. You made a great choice."

He moved closer and Anna wondered if he didn't feel Gemma's gaze burning into him. "What can I do for you today?" she asked as she turned to neaten the display of yarn to her left.

"I heard you had dinner with the new sheriff's deputy the other night."

Her hand stilled and she cringed inwardly. Of course, people had seen her and Lucas at the restaurant. And some of them had talked. It was what people did. It wasn't a small-town-only pastime, but living in a place where you knew everybody made it easier to notice what they were up to. She turned to Kyle. "I hope you haven't been gossiping about me." She tempered the words with a warm smile.

His ears turned pink. "Not gossiping," he said. "But I figured maybe it meant you'd changed your mind about dating. So I thought I'd ask again if you wanted to have dinner with me."

She pressed her lips together, buying time to think of kinder words than the ones that first came to mind; that who she went out with was none of his business and he should be gracious and accept no for an answer. Now she was probably going to end up hurting his feelings. "Thank you for the invitation, Kyle, but I'm not interested in having dinner with you." She forced herself to meet and hold his gaze as she spoke.

"How did you even meet that deputy?" he asked.

We met when I had a meltdown while my husband was dying, she might have said. Or, *We met when my late husband's best friend died.* Neither was an auspicious circumstance to begin a closer acquaintance. "It doesn't matter," she said.

He frowned. "I hope you know if you're ever afraid of anything or need protecting, you don't need to call a cop. You can call me."

What an odd thing to say. "Who do you think I need protecting from?" she asked.

He shrugged. "Somebody told me they saw that cop at your house last night. In uniform and everything. I thought that meant you called him about something, but maybe you invited him there for something else."

She drew herself up straight and made her voice frosty. "What I do in my own time is none of your business." Then, to avoid continuing the increasingly awkward conversation, she grabbed a ball of yarn from the display. "Mary Louise, you have to see this new mohair and silk blend we just got in."

A frequent customer, Mary Louise obligingly examined the ball of yarn Anna thrust at her, and they discussed the projects that might work well with the weight and fiber content of it. Anna smiled and nodded, and pretended to be fully engaged in the conversation, but she was too aware of the sound of the door slamming as Kyle exited the store.

Mary Louise ended up buying ten balls of the silk and mohair blend to knit a sweater, while her friend purchased the makings for a baby blanket. When they were gone, Gemma came to stand beside Anna at the cash register. "Kyle didn't look too happy when he left," she said.

"No, he wasn't." Anna turned toward her, arms folded. "He heard I had dinner with Lucas and decided that meant I was ready to date again."

"You mean he thought you were ready to date him," Gemma said.

"Yes. And now he's angry because I turned him down." She sighed. "Nothing I can do about that, but now things are going to be awkward between us, and I hate that."

"I bet you turned down a lot of men before you met Jonas," Gemma said.

"What makes you say that?"

"Because you're very pretty, but you're also particular," Gemma said. "And I mean that as a compliment. Unless I'm wrong, you weren't the type of social butterfly who accepts all invitations."

"You're right," Anna said. "I did pick and choose. I guess I'm out of practice letting men down easily."

"I hope Lucas Malone knows how lucky he is," Gemma said. She picked up a box of pattern books and carried them to the display at the front of the store.

Anna tidied the counter and thought about what Gemma had said. She hadn't hesitated to accept Lucas's invitation to dinner. Why was that? Why did she find him so attractive when other men left her cold?

Anna turned the sign on the front door of the shop to Closed shortly before six and swung by her house to drop off Jacquie before heading to Mo's pub. No sinister note greeted her today and, while Jacquie wasn't happy about being left behind, she didn't sense anything unusual about the house.

At Mo's, Anna made her way through the happy hour crowd to the table where Sandy waited. "Thanks for suggesting this," she said as she shed her coat.

"I wanted to talk to you," Sandy said. A server delivered a glass of beer and asked Anna what she would like.

"A glass of pinot noir," Anna said. When they

were alone again, she asked, "What did you want to talk to me about?"

Sandy didn't answer right away. She took a drink of beer and studied Anna for so long that Anna began to feel uncomfortable. She wore an oversized fisherman's sweater Anna thought might have belonged to Dave, and her short-cropped hair looked freshly cut. Pearly earrings and a sweep of dark mascara added a feminine touch. "I heard Lucas Malone was at your house last night," Sandy finally said.

Anna flinched. "Who told you that?"

"Don't be so jumpy. Alma Bettinger, who lives down the street from you, was in the bakery today and she said a sheriff's department SUV was parked in your driveway and a very good-looking cop—her words, not mine—was asking questions of all the neighbors. He wanted to know if they had seen anyone around your house that day while you were at work."

Anna hugged her arms over her stomach. "Someone left a note on my door. A note like the one you received, with the words cut from magazines."

"What did it say?"

"It said, 'Mind your own business or you'll be the next to die.'"

"Huh." Sandy sat back. "Why would anyone threaten you?"

"I don't know."

"Do they think you're connected to me or something?" Sandy asked.

"I don't know." She waited while the server set a

coaster and a glass of red wine in front of her, thanked her then took a sip.

"You worked that rescue last Saturday with George Anton," Sandy said.

"Yes."

"Did you say anything to him about me or Dave?"

"No. I didn't even talk to him." She hesitated then added, "I asked my brother-in-law about Anton. Justin has a restaurant in Junction. Red Mesa. He knows Anton. He told me he's signed a contract with him to supply his restaurant."

"What did your brother-in-law have to say about him?"

"That he made a good deal and has a good reputation."

She nodded. "That's true. I mean, Dave said he checked the guy out before he signed that contract. It just didn't work out for us the way it does most people."

"Why didn't it?" Anna asked. "I mean, if Anton loaned you the money to expand, it was in his best interest to make sure you got enough business to pay him back."

"If I knew the answer to that, I wouldn't be in this fix." She set aside her empty beer glass and signaled the server for another one. "Did Lucas say what the cops have found out so far? No one at the sheriff's department will tell me anything."

"He said he looked through Dave's office and didn't find anything."

"Yeah, he was there half the day. At least he was neat about it. We talked about you."

"You did?" Anna tried not to sound alarmed.

"I told him not to fall for you, that you're still married to Jonas."

"Jonas is dead," Anna said.

"Yeah, but you still feel married to him, don't you? No sense in a guy like Malone wasting time with you when there's so many women in this town who are desperate to hook up with a man."

Were those the only two categories of women Sandy saw—desperate and unavailable? "I will always love Jonas," she said. "But that doesn't mean I couldn't love someone else, too."

"Still, I can't really see you with a cop. Maybe a professor or a librarian or something."

"Jonas wasn't a professor or a librarian."

Sandy shrugged. "You were younger when you met him. Less set in your ways."

I am not set in my ways. Anna took a large swallow of wine to keep from saying this out loud. She hadn't come here to argue with Sandy, and she didn't like being put on the defensive.

Instead, she forced her shoulders to relax and smiled in a way she hoped was enigmatic. "I guess we'll just have to see," she said. "How are you doing? I know you've got a lot of arrangements to make. I found all the paperwork involved when a spouse dies a little daunting."

"I'm still waiting for the county to release the body."

"Are you using Hawkins and White for the arrangements?" Anna asked. "They were very helpful with planning Jonas's service."

"I'm not going to have a service," Sandy said.

"You're not?"

Sandy accepted a second beer from the server. "I'm not into that sort of thing and neither was Dave. I'm going to have him cremated and I'll scatter the ashes in the mountains somewhere this spring."

Anna started to argue that Dave's friends would welcome the opportunity to acknowledge his passing, but she kept back those words, too. This wasn't her decision to make. Maybe Sandy, as strong as she was outwardly, didn't want the pain of a formal ceremony and all those condolences. "That sounds very meaningful," she said instead.

"I got an offer on the house today. I still have to wait on the death certificate and some other paperwork, but the buyer isn't in a hurry."

"That was fast."

"It's a hot market. I still have to sell the business, but I'm hopeful I'll clear enough to pay what we owe."

Apparently, Sandy had decided against skipping out on her bills. She sounded so calm. Anna would have been devastated to have to leave her home and give up her livelihood. "What will you do then?" she asked.

"I might travel for a while, or go down to Mexico and hang out. I've got money of my own tucked away, so I'll be all right."

Anna tried to hide her shock. "Oh. That's nice." If Sandy had money, why was she selling everything?

Maybe it was family money, or tied up in a trust or something.

Sandy smirked. "You didn't think I was going to let George Anton and the bank have everything did you?"

So much for thinking she was hiding her feelings from this woman. "A fresh start will be good," she said.

"It will, but I can't go anywhere until the sheriff's department finishes their investigation."

"Knowing who killed Dave won't bring him back, but it has to be terrible, not knowing," Anna said.

"At this point I don't really care if they rule his death murder or suicide, I just want everything settled." She drained the beer then took out her wallet. "Tell your boyfriend to hurry it up so I can get on with my life," she said, setting a twenty-dollar bill on the table.

"He's not my—"

Sandy laughed. "Gotcha!" she said and walked away.

Anna stared at her half-full glass of wine, cheeks hot. Sandy had always made her uncomfortable, but it was worse now without Dave and Jonas to serve as buffers. "She just has a different sense of humor," Jonas had told Anna once. "Don't take anything she says personally."

Except it was hard not to feel like a target when Sandy took it upon herself to warn off the first man Anna had been interested in since Jonas had died.

She remembered Lucas's remark when he'd seen

Jonas's picture on the refrigerator. Anna had said she would always love him. She had thought he was acknowledging that bond with a loved one who is gone—the same bond he shared with his girlfriend who had died. But, really, he must have been alluding to Sandy's statement that Anna was still too tied to Jonas to be open to another relationship.

Six months ago, that might have been true, but not now. She ought to call Lucas and tell him so.

Before she could gather the nerve, another thought occurred to her. Maybe Lucas had brought up her love for Jonas as a way of letting her know he wasn't ready to move on from his relationship with Jenny. The idea settled in her stomach like a lead weight. Maybe he wasn't the one who needed to be warned off—she was.

Anna drained the glass of wine and thought about ordering another. Instead, she took out her wallet to pay. Better to go home to her dog and her knitting and keep things the way they had been. Quiet. Comfortable.

Lonely.

ON WEDNESDAY, Lucas drove to Junction to see George Anton. The office for Anton's Finest was a single-story, red-brick building in an industrial park next door to a cemetery. Lucas was surprised when Shaylin Brown came to the reception desk to greet him. "I didn't expect to see you, Ms. Brown," he said. "I thought you'd still be recovering from your accident."

She looked down at the navy blue sling on her left

arm, a cast visible inside the sling. "I'm still dealing with this thing, but that doesn't mean I can't work. George is so busy, he needs all the help he can get."

She led the way down a hallway. A trim brunette in a tailored gray pantsuit, she moved briskly, heels making muffled taps on the low-pile carpet. She opened a door near the end of the hallway and George Anton rose from the head of a conference table. "Hello, Deputy," he said. "Have a seat and we'll take care of this as quickly as possible."

The three of them sat at the table and Lucas took out his recorder and notepad. "I just have a few questions," he said.

"Of course." Anton folded his hands in front of him, relaxed. "Though I'm surprised Rayford County would send someone all the way to Junction to answer questions about a traffic accident. We could have done this on the phone."

"This isn't about the accident," Lucas said. "I need to ask you some questions about your relationship to Dave and Sandy Weiss."

Anton and Shaylin exchanged looks. "What about them?" Anton asked.

"Where were you on March 13?" Lucas asked.

Anton frowned. "I was a lot of places that day. Calling on clients. Here at the office some, I imagine. Why is that important?"

"I'll need a list of all the places you were on that day," Lucas said.

"Why?"

Lucas met the older man's confused gaze. "Dave Weiss died that day."

"He killed himself," Anton said. "I heard. I'm sorry, but I don't see what that has to do with me."

"Dave owed you a lot of money. He wasn't going to be able to pay you back."

"Are you saying that's why he killed himself? Did he leave a note that said that?"

"I just need the list of your whereabouts."

Anton looked to Shaylin. "Get my datebook, would you?" he asked.

She left the room and Anton turned back to Lucas. "I'm old-fashioned. I still like to keep things on paper." He ran a hand over his almost-bald head. "This is the first I've heard that Dave wasn't going to be able to pay me back," he said. "He was making the payments. He was bringing in plenty of money."

Shaylin returned and handed Anton a slim black notebook. Anton flipped through the pages, then ran his hand along one to flatten it, and passed it to Lucas. "It's all right there."

Lucas made note of the list of appointments. Anton had spent the morning at the office in a meeting with at least three other people, including Shaylin, and the rest of the day calling on clients, including Justin Trent.

He returned the notebook to Anton. "Mrs. Weiss said you financed the expansion of their business. Was that usual?"

"Sure. I like dealing with small businessmen like myself. I try to give them a break. It's a good investment. I can offer my restaurant clients a really quality product that is truly local. They get to advertise that they're supporting local growers and producers, and I'm supporting the little guy instead of some faceless corporation. It's a win all around. And all legal. I keep the two businesses separate, you see? I don't want any trouble with the IRS. It's all on the level, I promise. I have a team of lawyers and tax people who look over every contract to make sure it's so."

"How did that work for the Weisses?" he asked.

"The same way it works for any other supplier I deal with. I give them a good interest rate and scale the loan to the amount of business I project I can throw their way."

"What happens if your projections are off?" Lucas asked.

"They aren't." Anton tucked the notebook into his suit pocket. "I've been doing this a while now. I know what the market will bear."

"Sandy Weiss says they weren't getting enough income from you to make their sales."

"Maybe you misunderstood her. I can show you the figures. Here." He swiveled his chair and took a laptop computer from the credenza behind them. "It will just take me a minute to boot this up."

"I can ask Lisa to bring in some coffee or water, if you'd like," Shaylin said.

"No, thank you," Lucas said. He watched as Anton typed rapidly then began swiping at the screen.

Anton turned the computer toward Lucas. "That's the last six months' figures for Weiss Bakery," he said.

Lucas studied the spreadsheet on the screen, which showed amounts in the thousands to ten thousands for each month. It was a lot of money. "But what do they owe?" he asked.

Anton swung the laptop toward himself once more and scrolled again. "There." He angled the computer to Lucas again. "That's their note. See—they owed under half of their net take from me. Plenty left over for a little profit. And they still had all the income from their regular bakery and catering business."

Lucas made note of the figures. "This doesn't match with what Sandy Weiss told me," he said.

"Maybe her husband told her he wasn't making enough money because he was skimming money for something else," Shaylin said. "Drugs or gambling or an affair. A lot of women are completely ignorant of their husband's businesses."

"Not Sandy," Anton said. "If anything, she was more involved in this stuff than he was."

"Are you saying Sandy Weiss was involved in this contract?" Lucas asked.

"He signed it, because the business was all in his name, but she handled all the bookkeeping over there. I transferred the money I owed them into their account by electronic transfer every month and she paid me what they owed on their loan in a handwritten check. Her signature was on the checks."

"Sandy said Dave didn't like to use computers."

"That's right." Anton nodded. "I hesitated to do business with him because of that. It's too easy for things to get lost in the shuffle without computer records. But clients had been asking about his baked goods—his reputation was that good, so I took a chance. And they never missed a payment or screwed up an order. If anything, they were too generous. They were always throwing in extra things for the clients to try or sending goodies for the staff. People loved it, though."

"What about your contract with Justin Trent?"

Anton's gaze sharpened. "What about it? He doesn't have anything to do with the Weisses, does he?"

"I'm just wondering how an agreement with a supplier differs from your agreements with restaurants."

"I don't loan money to any restaurants," Anton said. "And the profit margins might be different. That's confidential information."

"I understand. I'm just trying to get a feel for how you operate."

"How do you know Justin?" Shaylin asked.

"I'm friends with his sister-in-law. She mentioned he works with your company."

"Yeah, I've known Justin a long time," Anton said. "Shaylin used to work for him. That's how we met."

"Back to the Weisses," Lucas said. "Someone sent Sandy Weiss a threatening letter, and she received some phone calls threatening her, too. Do you know anyone who would do something like that?"

"No. You think it was me? Why would I threaten her?"

"What about Anna Trent?" he asked. "She received a threatening letter, too."

"Is she related to Justin Trent? I've never met her. Never heard of. I sure didn't send her any letter."

"What kind of threat?" Shaylin asked.

"The letter writer threatened to kill these women," Lucas said.

Shaylin looked horrified. "That's terrible."

"I don't know anything about any letters," Anton said. He closed the laptop. "I don't know what else I can tell you."

"Thank you," Lucas said. "I appreciate your co-operation."

He stood and Shaylin rose, also. "I'll show you out."

Chapter Eleven

Shaylin Brown led the way back down the hall, through the reception area and out the front door. Then she turned and said, "Anna Trent is Justin's sister-in-law, isn't she?"

"Yes."

"I remember when she used to come into the restaurant, though we were never introduced." She rubbed one hand down the lapel of her suit. "She probably told you already that Justin and I had an affair. He ended it when his wife found out."

"She mentioned it when she saw you at the accident."

"She was there?"

"She's a volunteer with Search and Rescue."

"Those people are amazing." She shook her head. "Anyway, I just wanted you to know that George is telling you the truth when he says he doesn't know her. He knew Justin because Red Mesa has been in town for years, but I'm the one who talked Justin into signing with us. We're not together anymore, but we're still friends. And Justin knows a good deal when he sees it."

"Do you know anything about Dave Weiss's death?" Lucas asked. "Maybe something you didn't want to say in front of George?"

"No. I never met him. I never met Sandy, either, until the day of the accident. George wanted me to go along on the visit because Sandy's husband had just died and he thought it would be easier with another woman along. I think he was afraid she'd start crying or something." She rolled her eyes. "You know how some men are about tears."

"How did the meeting go?" Lucas asked.

"It went fine. Sandy was very composed, all business." Her eyes met his. "I'm not going to give you any details, but I will say she seemed happy with the business arrangement her husband had made and gave no indication she wanted to end the deal."

"She told you she wanted to continue the deal."

"Yes. On the same terms. She seemed happy about that."

That didn't match with what Sandy had told Anna about wanting to get out from under the debt. He made a mental note to check with Sandy about this.

"Is George in trouble?" Shaylin asked.

"If his alibi checks out, Mr. Anton has nothing to worry about," Lucas said.

"We heard that Dave Weiss killed himself— Sandy even sent a message to George saying that. But now you think it was murder?"

"We don't know. It's important to follow up on everything."

"I thought Eagle Mountain was such a pretty

town," she said. "Very peaceful. Now I hear there are people being threatened and possibly murdered. I guess looks really are deceptive." She rubbed her shoulders, as if chilled.

"When will you see Mrs. Weiss again?"

"George is going to see her tomorrow. I'm sure he'll ask her why she told you he wasn't paying them enough money to manage the loan. That isn't true. George is a very smart businessman, but he really does care about people."

And you care about him, Lucas thought. "Thank you for your help," he said. "I won't keep you any longer."

She took a step back. "Right. I hope you find whatever you're looking for."

So did he. Though it would help if he had a clearer idea of who or what that was.

After talking to Anton and Shaylin, Lucas stopped by the sheriff's department in Junction to say hello. "How's life in the mountains?" his good friend, Del Alvarez greeted him. "Are you tired of ticketing jaywalkers and putting cows back in pastures, and ready to deal with real crime again?"

"Actually, I'm working a really interesting case," Lucas said. "A possible murder."

"Possible?" Del raised an eyebrow in question.

Lucas outlined the particulars of the case. "Do you know anything about George Anton?" he asked.

"Never heard of him," Del said. "Does he have a rap sheet?"

"Nothing. Nobody in this case has anything worse than a parking violation."

"So maybe your guy really did commit suicide," Del said.

"Maybe." Lucas crossed his arms. "It just feels off. The more questions I ask, the more things don't add up."

"Don't let it get to you," Del said. "Sometimes we just don't have enough information to solve every case."

"I know."

"And I know you," Del said. "You don't let go of things. That can be good and bad." He slapped Lucas on the back. "Walk out with me. I have to get going."

They said goodbye in the parking lot.

Lucas checked the time and decided to have lunch before he headed back to Eagle Mountain. He drove to a mom-and-pop café downtown that had become a favorite over the years. He was walking up to the door when it opened and a woman with long dark hair emerged. She stopped abruptly when she saw him.

"Lucas!"

"Hello, Tanya." Jenny's sister looked enough like Lucas's former girlfriend to cause a tightness in his chest, but her expression was anything but friendly. "How are you?" he asked. She and Jenny had been close, and the last time he had seen her, a few days after Jenny's funeral, she had been devastated by grief.

"I'm better," she said. "I've been seeing someone. A therapist, I mean. She's helping me come to terms with everything that happened."

"That's good."

"It is." She started to move past him then stopped. She was close enough to touch him now and her gaze burned into him. "She told me I needed to forgive you for what you did to Jenny."

He opened his mouth to speak but she held up her hand. "I don't want to hear your self-justification," she said. "Just know I'm working on this. If Jenny could forgive you, I ought to be able to."

He hadn't intended to defend himself. He probably would have said something like, *I'm sorry every day about how things turned out.* Now, he could only say, "Thank you."

"Don't thank me. I'm doing this for my own mental health, not yours."

She moved on, hurrying to her car. Lucas pulled open the door to the café and went inside, shaken by the encounter. He ordered at the counter and carried his food to a booth, then stared out the window, not eating. He and Jenny used to come here, in the early days, when they were happy.

They came here the day they'd moved in together, after spending hours carrying furniture and unpacking boxes. He had been happy about the move, looking forward to seeing more of her.

He hadn't realized she had seen this as the first step toward marriage. Two years later, she had finally confronted him. "Are we going to get married?" she had asked.

The question hadn't surprised him. Jenny had been hinting for months that she wanted to make their relationship more permanent. He had gone so far as to visit a jewelry store to look at rings, but in the end, he couldn't buy one. "I love you," he'd told her. "But I'm not ready for marriage." Marriage was forever, and he wasn't sure his feelings for Jenny were that strong. Part of him was ashamed to admit it, but he'd known that he'd needed to be honest with her.

That had been a horrible night. Almost as horrible as two months later, when they learned she had cancer. She had been preparing to move out of their apartment and start dating other people, but her diagnosis had stopped everything. Lucas had committed to sticking by her through her treatment and, they hoped, her recovery. But the treatments didn't stop the disease.

Tanya had come to him near the end and suggested he marry Jenny anyway. "It's all she ever wanted," Tanya had said. "I think it's the least you could do to make her last days happier."

So he had bought a ring and gotten down on his knees in front of Jenny's wheelchair and proposed. She had looked at him, tears streaming down her face. "If it wasn't right nine months ago, it isn't right now," she'd said. She had put her hand on his shoulder. "I appreciate the gesture, but I think we both know we're better friends than we ever were lovers. You've showed that all these months, standing by me, and that means more to me than a ring or a wedding."

Jenny had forgiven Lucas for not loving her enough to marry her. But he was still a long way from forgiving himself. And now there was Anna.

He was so attracted to her, and she seemed to respond the same way. But he could feel the ghosts of her late husband and Jenny standing between them. He didn't know how to get past that, or if Anna even wanted to.

He was contemplating all this, his food growing cold, when his phone rang. He checked the screen and answered quickly. "Hello, Sheriff."

"Are you on your way back from Junction?" Travis asked.

"I'm finishing lunch and headed that way," Lucas said. He gathered up the uneaten food as he talked.

"Get here as soon as you can. Someone shot out the windows in the bakery."

WEDNESDAY MORNING, just before noon, a tall young man with a long blond ponytail came into Yarn and More. Three women were shopping at the time and they all stopped to stare as he moved through the shop.

"Hey, Anna!" He grinned when he saw her. "Is now a good time to talk about those shelves you want?"

"Now is perfect." Anna set aside the patterns she had been collating for an upcoming Knit Your First Sweater class and stood. "Thanks for stopping by, Bobby. I know a small job like this isn't usually worth your time."

"Anything for you." Bobby Fitch had worked for Jonas for two years before Jonas died, and he and his wife had ended up buying most of the business tools and equipment from Anna. "Do you have a sketch of what you want?"

"I do." She turned back to the worktable and shuffled through a pile of papers until she found the one she wanted. "I want a whole wall of shelves, on the diagonal, like this." She indicated the X-shaped pattern of boards she had drawn on a sheet of notepaper. "I want to end up with all these cubbies where I can stash yarn."

Bobby studied the paper then looked at the wall she indicated. "Oh, sure, we can do that," he said. "Do you want the wood painted or stained?"

"Stained, to match the other wood in here." She indicated the mahogany trim around the windows and doors. "And then over here." She turned to indicate a narrower space next to the checkout counter. "Here, I want vertical shelves for books. They need to be spaced fairly far apart—eighteen inches. A lot of needlework books are tall, and I can display other things there, too."

Bobby nodded. "Oh, sure. I can do that, too." He folded the sketch and tucked it into the front pocket of his denim work shirt. "I'll get you an estimate in a day or two. Or Melody will. That's her forte."

"No rush," Anna said. "I know you're busy."

"We are. It's been great." His expression sobered. "I owe you and Jonas everything, giving me this chance. Not many guys my age have their own business."

"You deserve it," she said. "Jonas would be so proud." She blinked rapidly, eyes stinging and her throat tight.

"Thanks. Hey, I've been meaning to ask you. What

happened to that old Dodge Dart Jonas had in his garage?"

The reference to the Dart surprised her. "It's still in the garage," she said. "Jonas never finished it." He had never had time.

"If you ever want to sell it, I'd make you a good offer," Bobby said.

"I didn't know you were interested in old cars."

"Kind of." He shrugged. "That one was special anyway. Because it belonged to Jonas."

She nodded. "I'll let you know if I ever decide to sell it," she said.

"It was good to see you again." He patted his pocket. "Melody or I will call you with that estimate."

He strode out of the business and Anna exhaled. The shoppers went back to examining skeins of yarn and Gemma finished adding up a customer's purchase.

Anna's phone rang and she was surprised to see the call was from Sandy. "Anna, I'm sorry to bother you," Sandy said. "I know you're at work."

Sandy didn't sound like herself. Her voice vibrated with tension. "You're not bothering me," Anna said. "What's wrong?"

"I was here at the bakery, working in the office. There weren't any customers, and I heard this…this explosion. I ran into the front room and glass was everywhere, and tires squealed as someone drove away."

"Sandy, what happened?" Anna fought back alarm.

"Someone shot out the front window. The one with the Weiss Bakery sign." Sandy choked back a sob. "I could have been killed."

"Did you call the sheriff?" Anna asked.

"Yes. They're on their way."

"I'm coming, too," Anna said.

"Thanks," Sandy said. "I didn't know who else to call."

"I'll be there in a few minutes. Just hang on."

She looked up to find two of the shoppers and Gemma staring at her, open-mouthed. "Someone shot out the window of the bakery?" Gemma asked.

Anna stared at her. "How did you know?"

Gemma shrugged. "Sandy talks pretty loud. And I have good hearing."

Anna pocketed the phone. "I need to go over there. She's frantic and the sheriff's deputies are on their way."

"Go," Gemma said. "We can handle it here. That poor woman has certainly had more than her share of bad luck."

She had, Anna agreed. But was it really bad luck that plagued the Weisses or something much more sinister and dangerous?

Chapter Twelve

Lucas recognized Anna's car ahead of him as he turned onto the dead-end street leading to Weiss Bakery. A trio of sheriff's department SUVs were already pulled up in front of the building, and the parking lot was strung with yellow crime-scene tape. Anna parked on the side of the road and skirted the tape as she made her way toward the front door.

Lucas jogged to catch up with her. "Anna, what are you doing here?" he asked.

She stopped and waited. She wore some kind of knitted wrap that gathered in folds around her neck, framing her face and drawing attention to her full lips and wide-spaced eyes. "Sandy called me," she said. "She sounded terrified."

She looked past him, toward the front of the bakery, and he turned to take in the large front window, several big shards of glass still hanging from the wooden frame, more glass glittering in the gravel of the parking lot. Sandy stood in front of the door with the sheriff and Deputy Dwight Prentice. She wore a stained blue apron over jeans and a green sweatshirt.

Sandy looked up as Anna and Lucas approached, her face blotchy, as if she'd been crying. "I got here as soon as I could," Anna said.

"I shouldn't have called you," Sandy said. "I don't know what I was thinking. It was just…"

"You were upset and you didn't want to be alone," Anna said. "That's perfectly natural."

"Hello, Anna," Travis said. "Would you take Sandy inside while we finish processing the scene?"

"Of course." Anna stepped forward and took Sandy's arm. "Let's go into your office."

Lucas waited until the women were inside with the door shut before he spoke. "What happened?" he asked.

"Sandy says she was in her office, getting ready to eat the sandwich she had brought from home for her lunch, when she heard tires on the gravel in the parking lot," Dwight said. "She started toward the front, thinking she had a customer, but before she had taken three steps, the front window exploded. She screamed and hit the floor and whoever fired the shot drove away. By the time she got to her feet and looked out the door, whoever had done this was gone."

"Just one shot?" Lucas asked.

"Just one." Travis held up an evidence bag with a spent shotgun shell. "Number 9 birdshot. This was lying in the parking lot."

Dwight looked around them. "There aren't any other businesses on this street and the closest house is two blocks away," he said. "We'll ask around, but the person who did this probably knew they wouldn't be seen."

"Did Sandy get a description of the vehicle?" Lucas asked.

"No. I asked if she had had any new threats, and she said no," Travis said. "She didn't have any customers here at the time, and no one had come in either the half hour before or the few minutes after the shot was fired."

"We don't have much to go on," Dwight said. "The ammo is pretty common. There aren't any tracks in the gravel lot. No cameras. No neighbors or customers to hear anything."

"Did you talk to George Anton?" Travis asked.

"I did. He says he never threatened the Weisses. And he said their proceeds from the bakery sales to him were more than enough to cover their loan payments. He showed me figures on his computer that backed up this claim. He gave me his schedule for the day Dave Weiss died. I still need to check that out, but if it holds, I don't see how he could have been involved in Dave's death."

"He could have hired someone to do it," Dwight said.

"But why would he?" Travis asked. He glanced at the broken window again. "What time did you talk to him?" he asked.

"I was with him from eleven to about eleven twenty," Lucas said.

"It's just possible he could get here from Junction

in forty minutes," Travis said. "Call him right now and see what he says."

Lucas tried George Anton's number but the call went to voice mail. Then he dialed Shaylin Brown. She answered on the second ring. "Hello?"

"This is Deputy Lucas Malone. I'm trying to reach George and he's not answering his phone."

"He turns off his phone when he's in a meeting," she said.

"Can you tell me who he's meeting with?" Lucas asked.

"Sure. Hang on a sec." A long beat of silence then she was back on the line. "He's meeting with Justin Trent."

"Thank you."

"Is there anything I can help you with?" she asked.

"No. Just routine follow-up." He ended the call and looked up the number for Red Mesa. A woman answered. Lucas identified himself and asked to speak to Justin Trent. Moments later, a man came on the line.

"Hello?"

"Mr. Trent, is George Anton there?" Lucas asked.

"He just left. Why?"

"How long was he with you?"

"We had lunch together. Why is a Rayford County Sheriff's deputy interested in George Anton?"

"It's just routine. How long was Mr. Anton with you?"

"Almost two hours," Trent said. "Does this have anything to do with Anna?"

"No, sir, it does not. Thank you for your time." Lucas ended the call. "Justin Trent says George Anton was with him for the last two hours."

"Let's have another word with Sandy," Travis said.

Anna and Sandy sat across from each other in the office. Both women looked up when the three men entered. "You can go now, Anna," Travis said.

"No," Sandy said. "I want her to stay." She glanced at Anna. "You'll stay, won't you?"

"Of course." Anna adjusted the knitwear around her neck.

Travis pulled a folding chair over in front of the women and sat. "What haven't you told us?" he asked.

Sandy stared. "I don't know what you're talking about."

"I'm looking at this picture..." Travis said. "Your husband dead under mysterious circumstances. Debts that don't fit Dave's historic behavior. Anonymous phone calls and a couple of threatening notes that look like something out of a kids' book. A drive-by shooting that on the surface appears unprovoked. We're missing too much information. Things you haven't told us."

"I've told you everything I know," she said.

"Tell us more about this debt," Travis said. "George Anton says you were earning more than enough from the meat contract to make the payments on the loan he extended you for improvements to your business."

"He's lying." The muscles along her jaw tightened.

"Had Dave borrowed any other money?" Travis

asked. "Was he involved with loan sharks? Was he into drugs?"

Her face paled, freckles standing out across her nose. "Drugs?"

"Maybe he was siphoning off money to feed his habit?" Travis asked. Lucas wondered what Travis was getting at. The autopsy on Dave Weiss hadn't showed any sign of drug use, other than the dog tranquilizers, and they certainly weren't a commonly abused substance.

"No. How can you say such a thing?" Sandy buried her face in her hands and began to sob, loud, shaking sobs. Sandy Weiss had been stoic to this point, almost emotionless at times. This sudden weeping shocked them all into silence.

Anna leaned over and put a hand on Sandy's shoulder. "I think you've upset her enough," she said and frowned at them.

Travis stood. "We'll leave for now," he said. "But we may want to talk to you again."

The men filed out. Lucas paused in the doorway to look back, hoping to catch Anna's eye, but she was focused on Sandy, murmuring something to her, so softly he couldn't make out the words.

He followed the sheriff and Dwight back into the parking lot. "You didn't come up with anything suspicious when you searched the office here?" Travis asked.

"No, sir." He rubbed the back of his neck. "Maybe if we could find Dave's phone…"

"His provider says they haven't been able to track

it," Travis said. "Which probably means it's been destroyed. I'm going to try to get a warrant to search the Weisses' home. I don't know if I'll succeed, but we need to find out more about what Dave was up to right before he died. Sandy isn't helping."

"She may not know," Lucas said.

"I have a feeling she does," Travis said. "But maybe she's trying to protect her husband's reputation." He shifted his gaze to Lucas. "You might suggest Anna be careful. If Dave was involved in something dangerous, she wants to watch her back. Maybe that threat someone left at her house was more serious than we thought."

Anna and Sandy sat in silence as the sheriff and his deputies got into their vehicles and drove away. Sandy let out a long breath as the noise of their tires on gravel faded. "Nothing like having the cops accuse you of lying to really cap off a horrible day," she said.

"They're frustrated because they aren't finding any more evidence," Anna said. "I don't think they really believe you're lying."

"The sheriff does." The desk chair creaked as Sandy shifted. "And he's not exactly wrong."

Anna stared. "What do you mean?"

"There is one thing I didn't tell them." Her eyes met Anna's, her gaze unblinking. "It's not anything that important. It may not even mean anything. But I think it's probably safer for me not to tell."

Anna sat again and leaned toward Sandy. "What is it?"

"When I saw George Anton on Saturday, I told him I was thinking of closing the business," Sandy said. "He got so upset when I mentioned it that I backed off. I pretended that I intended to keep things going, and to keep repaying the money he had loaned Dave, and keep supplying desserts to his restaurants. But I think he was suspicious."

"You should tell the sheriff this," Anna said. "It could be important. If George was upset about losing your business..."

"No." Sandy shook her head. "I can't say anything to the sheriff because of the other thing I didn't tell him."

Anna waited, holding her breath.

"George had a gun with him," Sandy said. "He wore it in a holster under his jacket, and he made a point of pulling back the jacket so I could see."

"What did he say?" Anna asked. "Did he threaten you?"

"He didn't say anything. I think he was letting that gun do the talking. And that's why I can't go to the sheriff. Shooting out my window is one thing, but the next time, the bullet might be meant for me."

"That's horrible." Anna gripped Sandy's hand. "You really need to tell the sheriff. You shouldn't be trying to deal with this on your own."

Sandy pulled her hand away and stood. "I am dealing with it. I'm going to sell everything and move to where George Anton can't find me. Until then, I'm going to make him think I'm going along with his plans. It's the only way."

Anna didn't agree, but this wasn't her decision to make. "Is there anything I can do to help?" she asked.

"Thanks for coming today," Sandy said. "The cops were probably easier on me because you were here." She laughed. "Your boyfriend's face when you gave them all the stink eye when they tried to question me was priceless. Like a hurt little boy."

"He's not my boyfriend," Anna said.

"You may not think so, but he does, and that's what counts." She picked up a stack of papers from the desk. "Before you go, let me give you something from the case up front. A treat to repay you for your trouble."

"You don't have to do that," Anna called after Sandy, who was already on her way to the front. Anna hurried to collect her coat and purse then followed Sandy to the front of the store.

"It's just a couple of cupcakes." Sandy turned to the counter behind the front case and arranged something in a small bakery box. "I know the chocolate ones with pink frosting are your favorite. Could you hand me that tape there on the top of the case?"

Anna searched and found the tape dispenser sitting on top of the glass case. "Here you go." She handed it to Sandy, who tore off a strip and sealed the box shut.

Sandy handed the box to Anna. "I need to get back to work and you probably do, too," she said. "Thanks, again."

"What about the window?" Anna asked. "You can't leave everything like it is."

"I've got some plywood in the back I can nail over it," Sandy said. "I'll have to close for a few days, but that will give me time to take care of some other things." She shrugged. "Don't worry about me. I can take care of myself."

Anna left, suddenly anxious to be away. She didn't understand Sandy, who was terrified one moment and completely calm and in charge the next. She didn't act like any friend Anna had ever had. Their only real connection was through their dead husbands. But Anna's loyalty to Dave and to Jonas kept her reaching out to Sandy. She didn't seem to have any other friends to rally round her, and she shouldn't have to go through all this alone.

Gemma was leading a sock-making class when Anna returned to the shop, so Anna didn't have to face immediate questions about what had happened. She fetched her lunch from the refrigerator in the storeroom and sat at the little café table to eat. The sandwich was chicken left over from some she had grilled a couple of days ago. She had taken the first bite when Gemma swept in. "The estimate for the shelves is on the table in the workroom," Gemma said.

"Thanks," Anna said. "Is the class over already?"

"The students are focused on turning the heels." Gemma slid into the chair across from Anna. "I've got a couple of minutes before they get frustrated and start calling for help. How is Sandy?"

"She's fine. Determined to be strong and not let anything get her down."

"That's Sandy," Gemma said. "She's not the kind of person I would ever feel I could confide in, but if I was ever stranded in the wilderness, she'd be a good person to have along. She'd know how to fix the car, find dinner, and navigate out of there. She's scary competent that way."

"She is," Anna agreed. Sandy had won awards with the fire department, and bragged that she was a better businessperson than Dave. She probably would know how to survive in the wilderness. But Anna wouldn't want to be stuck there with her. It was an ugly thought, but she wasn't so sure Sandy wouldn't go her own way and leave someone like Anna behind.

She looked down at her sandwich, her appetite gone. "I'll save the rest of this for tomorrow," she said and wrapped up the remains of her lunch before Gemma could comment on how little she had eaten. "Why don't we see how the students are doing on turning those heels?"

"It always confuses everyone at first," Gemma said.

"It does. Then when you figure it out, you feel like a genius," Anna said. She would ask Lucas if he ever felt that way when he solved a case.

That is, if they ever had that kind of conversation again. When he had left her house Monday night, he had seemed intent on putting some distance between them, as if he sensed her growing feelings for him and didn't want to encourage her. At the bakery this morning, he had been all business. What else could she expect, though, considering he was on duty and dealing with a serious matter? If only she could read him better.

For that matter, if only she could understand her own feelings. Apparently, romance didn't get any easier with age. She still felt like a teenager playing the will-he-won't-he guessing game. And she wasn't even sure what she wanted his answer to be.

Chapter Thirteen

Travis asked Lucas to come into his office when they got back to the sheriff's department after leaving the bakery. "What's your take on this?" Travis asked. His desk chair creaked as he leaned back.

Lucas sat in the visitor's chair across from the sheriff and tried not to squirm like a kid in the principal's office. He wanted to come up with some brilliant observation that proved he had insight into the whole case. But everything was a muddled mess in his mind. "Why would someone go after a small-town baker and his wife?" he asked.

Travis nodded. "Whatever is going on there, I don't think it started with those notes to Sandy. This goes back to before Dave died. Whether he took his own life or was murdered, I think it's connected to these threats."

"Shooting out the bakery window is escalating things," Lucas said.

"Sandy has the house for sale," Travis said. "She says it's because she needs to money to pay her debts.

George Anton says different, and he showed you figures to prove it."

"Maybe she owes money to someone else," Lucas said. "Someone she doesn't want to tell us about."

"Did you find anything in the bakery office about how much they owed and to whom?"

"No. She said the financial records are with their CPA and she wasn't in a hurry to provide them to me. Without a warrant, I couldn't press."

Travis sat up, elbows on the desk. "What if we're wasting all this time investigating what turns out to be a suicide?" he asked. "Was there a ladder at the bakery?"

"I looked around and didn't see one. And none at the house, either. In fact, she had already gotten rid of everything of Dave's—clothes, tools, everything in the garage and most of the furniture, too."

"Why is she in such a hurry?" Travis asked. "I keep coming back to that."

"Because she's grieving and can't stand to be in the house and business she shared with her husband," Lucas said.

"Maybe. Or because she's guilty of something and wants to leave before she's caught."

"Guilty of what?" Lucas asked. "I can't see her hauling a man Dave's size up a ladder in the middle of nowhere. And she hasn't gained anything from his death. If anything, she's going to lose everything."

"Then that takes us back to these threats," Travis said.

"She wants to leave Eagle Mountain before the

person who threatened her does to her what they did to her husband," Lucas said.

"Who's making the threats?" Travis asked. "George Anton?"

"Or someone he hired."

Travis drummed his fingers on the desktop. "What's his motive?"

"If we could find that out, we might have the answer to the whole case," Lucas said.

"Stay on Anton," Travis said. "Find out as much as you can. And we'll keep a close eye on Sandy, too. Maybe the person making threats has made other contact with her and she's too frightened to tell us."

Sandy had never appeared very frightened to Lucas, but he knew people could be hard to read. Behind her stoicism, she might be panicked. If Dave had been murdered, killing him had to have been difficult. His widow would make a much easier target.

ANNA NEEDED TO move to sort out her thoughts, so after work she took Jacquie for a long walk. While the dog sniffed at the bare branches of shrubs and rolled in the snow, Anna pondered what to do with the information Sandy had given her. The sheriff needed to know about this, and if something happened to Sandy because Anna had kept quiet, she would carry the guilt for the rest of her life. Sandy hadn't sworn her to secrecy. Reviewing the conversation, Anna even wondered if Sandy had told her the story about George Anton so that she would pass it on to Lucas.

She got home after seven. She had no idea what Lucas would be doing right now, but she called him anyway. If he didn't answer, she would leave a message asking him to call. But he answered quickly.

"Hello, Anna," he said. "How are you doing?"

"I'm fine," she said.

"I'm glad to hear it. I know our questions upset you," he said. "But it's our job to ask the hard questions. People lie, and those lies make it harder for us to help them."

"I know that," Anna said. She traced a finger through the dust on a side table. Past time she did a little housework. "Listen, about Sandy. You were right. There was something she wasn't telling you."

"What is that?" She sensed a new tension in his voice.

"I've been debating all evening whether or not to tell you. But Sandy didn't say I shouldn't, and she's wrong for not telling you herself. I told her so."

"What is it she didn't tell us?"

"She says at her meeting with George Anton last Saturday, he had a gun."

"What kind of gun?"

"A handgun," Anna said. "He was wearing it in a shoulder holster under his coat. He didn't exactly threaten her with it, but she said he made sure she saw it, and she felt it was a threat. She said he was upset because she told him she was going to sell the business and wouldn't be able to fulfill the contract Dave had signed."

"He didn't say anything about this when I talked to him yesterday."

"Later on, she said that she decided to pretend to go along with George, even though she plans to sell the business and leave town. Maybe he believes her."

"Anton couldn't have been the one who shot out her window," Lucas said. "He was meeting with Justin at the time."

Justin again. Why did one of her least favorite people keep popping up? Anna didn't know whether to laugh or shake her head in exasperation. "I can't get over all the ways everyone is connected. Does that happen in all your cases?"

"Sometimes. I'll talk to George again and see what he has to say. Thanks for telling me. You're helping Sandy, whether she appreciates it or not."

"I'm sure she doesn't appreciate it, but that doesn't matter," Anna said.

"I won't let Anton know how I got this information," he said. "But promise me you'll be careful. Call me if anything happens that seems unusual or unsettling."

"Now you're scaring me," she said.

"I don't mean to. I'm going to drive by later to check on your house. I won't stop, but I want you to know I'm out there."

His words warmed her. She started to tell him to stop by, but held back. Her feelings for Lucas—and his for her—weren't clear, and she didn't want to expect anything from either of them that they weren't ready to give. "Thank you," she said. "That makes me feel very safe."

Safe was good, but was it what she really wanted? Maybe it was time to think in terms of less safety and more adventure. Lucas might be the man she wanted as her guide.

GEORGE ANTON SAT behind his desk and didn't conceal his frustration with yet another round of questions from the deputy. "Yes, I own a handgun," he said. "No, I don't carry it around with me. And I've never threatened anyone with it."

Anton was dressed in a suit identical to the one Lucas had seen him in before. But today, Shaylin Brown wasn't with him. "So you weren't upset with Mrs. Weiss when she told you she was closing her bakery and wouldn't be able to fulfill the contract Dave Weiss made with you?" Logan asked.

Anton's scowl deepened. "Sandy Weiss told me she wanted to continue the contract. I'm supposed to pick up a new shipment of pastries from her next week. She never said anything about canceling the contract."

He planted both hands palms down on the desk, as if about to shove up out of his chair. "I don't know why she's telling you these lies. First, she told you I wasn't paying her and her husband enough for the baked goods they provided and that's why they were in debt. That's not true. I've showed you the numbers to prove it. And she told you she was closing the bakery and canceling her contract with me, but she told me she wanted to continue the contract and wanted it to be even bigger. She told you I was carrying a gun and I wasn't."

"What would she have to gain by lying about you?" Lucas asked.

"Nothing," Anton said. "But whether she wants to end our contract or not, I have the option of canceling it myself, and I'll do so if she keeps spreading these lies about me."

"Someone shot out the front window of Weiss Bakery yesterday afternoon," Lucas said.

"Is that why you're asking all these questions about a gun?" Anton shook his head. "I wasn't anywhere near Eagle Mountain yesterday."

"I'm aware of that," Lucas said. "Do you know anyone who might do such a thing?"

"No." He leaned forward. "Look, I'm sorry the woman lost her husband. I liked Dave Weiss. He was a good man, I think. But he was just one of my clients. If I lose one, I find someone else to take his place. I'm not going to waste time trying to bully someone into continuing to do business with me. It doesn't make any sense."

Lucas stood. "Thank you for your time, Mr. Anton."

Lucas left the office, but he didn't return to Eagle Mountain. He turned toward the center of town and Red Mesa. At just after eleven in the morning, the restaurant was already busy. A hostess in a sleeveless black blouse and slim trousers greeted him just inside the door. "One for lunch?" she asked with a welcoming smile.

"I need to see Justin Trent," he said.

The smile faltered and her gaze swept over his khaki uniform once more. "Wait just a moment, please."

While he waited, he studied the award commendations that filled the wall behind the hostess's stand. Best local eatery year after year from the local newspaper. An environmental award, and one from a regional food and wine publication. More diners entered and gave him curious looks before being led to tables by a second young woman.

Justin Trent was a slender man several inches shorter than Lucas, dressed in an expensive-looking suit and highly polished shoes, his dark hair gelled and slicked straight back. "What can I help you with, Deputy?" he asked.

"I have a few questions for you, Mr. Trent," Lucas said. "Can we talk somewhere private?"

A trace of a frown creased Trent's forehead before it was banished. "Come this way," he said and turned to lead him away from the dining room.

They passed through an empty bar area and through a door into a dark-paneled office with a polished wood desk and shelves filled with more awards. Trent leaned back against the desk and crossed his arms over his chest. "What's this about?"

"George Anton came to see you yesterday afternoon."

"Yes, I told you when you called that he had just left. What is this all about?"

"Does George Anton carry a gun?"

"A gun!" The word exploded in a bark. "I don't know. I've never seen him with a gun. Why would he?" He gripped the edge of the desk with both hands. "Has George shot someone?"

"Not that I'm aware of," Lucas said. "Do you know a woman named Sandy Weiss?"

"She's Dave Weiss's wife, isn't she? Widow now, I guess."

"How well do you know her?"

"Not at all. I may have met her once, but I don't recall. Dave was my brother Jonas's friend, not mine."

"The Weisses supplied desserts to George Anton," Lucas said. "I believe you contract with Anton, also."

"Yes. He supplies lots of restaurants. Meats, vegetables, baked goods, all from different local sources." He straightened. "Is George involved in something illegal? Because I want no part of it."

"There's nothing illegal going on that I'm aware of," Lucas said. "I'm just trying to understand the arrangement Anton had with the Weisses."

"I don't know anything about it," Trent said.

"Thank you for your time." Lucas turned to leave.

"Wait," Trent said.

Lucas faced him once more.

"Let me ask you a question," Trent said. "What do you know about drug trafficking in Junction?"

Lucas hid his surprise. "There's a drug problem here," he said. "Mostly opioids. That's no secret. It's a problem in a lot of places."

"One of my workers, a sous-chef who's been with me for five years, was arrested yesterday for dealing," Trent said. "He was caught red-handed, apparently. I had no clue." He shook his head. "He's been one of my best employees. Never a hint he was involved in drugs. His lawyer tells me he doesn't take them, but he says he came across a deal that was too good to pass up. An easy way to make a lot of money. When I first saw your uniform, I figured you were here to talk about him."

"What kind of deal?" Lucas asked.

"I don't know. He's not saying, apparently hoping to bargain his way to a lesser sentence. But now I'm worried he wasn't the only one involved. He was supposedly dealing out of this restaurant and I can't have that. I won't have it."

"Do you think this has some connection to George Anton?" Lucas asked.

"No! I just… I'm trying to find out everything I can and I thought you might know something."

"I'm sorry, I can't help you."

Trent nodded. He looked older, truly worried.

Lucas left the restaurant and took out his phone.

"You miss me so much you can't stay away, is that it?" Del said when he answered Lucas's call.

"That's it," Lucas said. "What can you tell me about a sous-chef from Red Mesa who was arrested yesterday for dealing drugs out of the restaurant?"

"I heard something about that," Del said. "But you need to talk to Detective Jacobs in Vice. That was her collar."

"Is she around today?"

"I just saw her."

"I'm on my way."

Ten minutes later, Del met him in the hallway outside the bullpen. "What's this about?" he asked.

"I'm looking into a connection with a case I have in Eagle Mountain," he said.

"I told Jacobs you were on your way over to see her," Del said. "You rated a big smile. Word is, she and the dude from the city that she was dating split up. You ought to ask her out."

Lucas shook his head. Detective Michaela Jacobs was a striking brunette with a wicked sense of humor. A few weeks ago, he would have been flattered to learn that he'd merited a smile from her. But a few weeks ago, he hadn't been interested in dating anyone. And he hadn't met Anna Trent.

"Lucas, when are you coming back to Junction?" Michaela looked up from her desk, smile set to dazzle. Yes, there was definite interest there. He was flattered but felt nothing in return.

"I should be back in a month or so," he said. "I won't keep you long. What can you tell me about this sous-chef from Red Mesa you arrested for dealing?"

"He's not the first restaurant employee we've pulled in." She sat back, all business now. "There's apparently a whole network of people working out of restaurants. But we haven't found their supplier, or even how they're getting the drugs."

"Any connection to a man called George Anton?"

Her eyebrows rose. "How do you know George?"

"I'm investigating a suspicious death in Eagle Mountain and his name has come up."

"We've been keeping an eye on George," she said. "He supplies every restaurant where we've made an arrest, but we can't find anything tying him to the drug smuggling. Do you think he killed this guy?"

"I don't have any evidence of that. The man who died was one of his suppliers."

"If you come up with any connection to drugs—fentanyl, mostly—let me know. The supply has really expanded in the past year and we think it's coming from this group of restaurants, but we can't pin anything down."

"I will."

She relaxed again and leaned forward. "Maybe we could get together next time you're in the area. I'll buy you a drink."

"Thanks," he said. "But I've sort of met someone. In Eagle Mountain."

She laughed. "'Sort of met'?"

"I've met her. We went out once, but it's a little complicated. She's a widow and maybe not ready to get involved yet."

"Then *maybe* you should ask her if she wants to get involved. With you." Michaela laughed again. "Good luck, Deputy. And if things don't work out with the widow, I'll still buy you that drink."

"How are things with you and Lucas?" Gemma asked as she and Anna sat down to eat lunch at the worktable Friday afternoon. The whine of a power drill and banging of hammers disturbed the normally peaceful vibe of the store, but Anna was thrilled to have her new shelves. Bobby had offered to come in after the store closed, but she hated to ask him to work late. In the meantime, she had hung a Construction in Progress, Watch Your Step sign on the door and retreated with Gemma to the table at the back of the front room.

"There is no 'thing' with me and Lucas," she said. They had eaten a couple of meals together. She liked talking to him. She liked kissing him. But a second kiss had never happened and, in any case, it was far too early for there to be any "thing" between them. She unwrapped her sandwich and frowned at it.

"How long has that been in the refrigerator here?" Gemma asked.

"Only a couple of days." She took a bite and chewed. The sandwich was a little dry, but she couldn't let it go to waste.

Gemma drizzled dressing on her salad. "Have they found whoever shot the window out of the bakery?" she asked.

"How would I know?"

"I thought Lucas might have said."

"Do you think all we talk about is his job?" They did talk about that a lot, but Gemma didn't have to know that.

"I hope not. When do you see him again?"

"You're really nosy, did you know that?" Anna said.

Gemma grinned. "I like to think of it as caring about my friends."

Gemma was a good friend, the kind you could

call on to listen to your problems, or help you bury a body. "I don't know when we'll see each other again," she said. "We're both very busy."

"If he doesn't call you, you should call him," Gemma said.

"Gemma."

She held up both hands, surrendering. "Okay, okay. I'll back off."

Bobby stuck his head around the shelf that divided the workspace from the rest of the store. "Want to come take a look?" he asked.

Anna abandoned the half-eaten sandwich and followed him up front, Gemma right behind her. The smell of sawdust and fresh wood stain almost overwhelmed the more familiar odor of wool, but the results were worth a little disruption to the store's usual atmosphere. "They're perfect," she said. She ran her hand along the smooth wood, picturing the diamond-shaped cubbies filled with colorful yarn skeins.

"I'm glad you like them," Bobby said. "We'll get out of your hair now."

"You're going to be able to display a lot of yarn with this design," Gemma said. "Do you know how you want to lay things out?"

"I have a plan." Anna started toward the front counter and the drawer where she had stashed her notebook. But she only took a couple of steps before the door opened and Lucas entered.

He was in his khaki uniform, sans leather coat as today was sunny and warmer. He removed his sunglasses and his brown eyes fixed on her. "Hi, Anna," he said.

"Hi, Lucas." They stood there, smiling at each other, but neither speaking. Anna felt a little like a girl with a crush—something she would have sworn she was far too old for, but apparently not.

"That's everything, then." Bobby picked up a plastic bin full of tools.

"Thank you so much," Anna said. "Everything looks perfect."

"No problem," he said. "Call me anytime you need anything. And let me know if you decide to sell the Dart."

Lucas watched him leave then turned back to Anna. "The Dart?" he asked.

"It's a car Jonas was fixing up. I probably should pass it on to someone who will care about it as much as he did." She moved closer to him and lowered her voice, though she knew Gemma was listening and would probably overhear every word. "What brings you here?"

"Turns out I have the night free. I know it's last minute, but would you like to have dinner?"

Yes! This is what she shouted inside. What she actually said was, "That sounds nice."

"Is six thirty too early?"

"Six thirty would be great." She would ask Gemma to close up and leave the shop early enough to change and get ready.

"Great. I'll see you then." He gave her a last long look, then turned and walked out.

"You may not think there's any 'thing' between you two, but his eyes said different." Gemma stepped out from behind the divider. "I'll close up the shop tonight," she said.

"Thanks." Anna squeezed Gemma's arms and walked back to the worktable, though really, she felt as if she were dancing or floating, carried along by this wonderful anticipation.

At five thirty, Gemma nagged Anna into leaving the shop. They had spent most of the afternoon arranging yarn in the new cubbies, and they weren't done yet. Everything they moved into the new display left a gap elsewhere that had to be filled. What Anna had envisioned as a few hours' work was clearly going to take much longer. "We can work on this more tomorrow," Gemma said. "Go. Make yourself gorgeous."

"I'm not aiming for gorgeous," Anna said. "Just moderately attractive."

"Don't sell yourself short," Gemma said. "You can definitely do gorgeous."

Anna laughed, snapped on Jacquie's lead, and she and the dog headed home.

At the house, she started toward her bedroom to shower and change, but took a detour to the kitchen, suddenly starving. The half a stale sandwich she had eaten for lunch had vanished long ago. She needed to eat something to tide her over until dinner was served.

She spotted the bakery box on the counter and her mouth watered. There was one cupcake left—

perfect. She opened the box and admired the pink-frosted cake then peeled off the wrapper and broke the cake in half. The one she had enjoyed yesterday was a plain chocolate cupcake, but this one was one of Dave's Surprise Cakes. A hollow inside the cake contained a swirl of rich chocolate ganache.

For nonedible surprises, Dave used a plastic capsule—the kind found in gum machines—to contain the charm, ring or other object. "I don't worry about anyone accidentally swallowing that big plastic capsule," he had explained to Anna when they were discussing the cakes for her and Jonas's wedding. "The last thing I need is someone suing me because their girlfriend accidentally ate her engagement ring."

The cupcakes for their wedding had contained silver charms that represented aspects of her and Jonas—a hammer and saw for him, knitting needles in a ball of yarn and a tiny pair of scissors for her. In her jewelry box, she kept a charm bracelet with all the different mementos from those desserts.

Smiling at the memory, she took a bite of the cupcake, letting the chocolate melt on her tongue. The cake was fresh, though she wondered if Sandy had gone a little overboard on the red food coloring in the frosting on top. Anna could taste the bitter chemical tang from the coloring. Still, the chocolate cake did a good job of making up for that. She finished the cake then deposited the bakery box in the trash, ready for the rest of her evening.

She showered and changed, fed Jacquie, then returned to her bathroom to do her makeup and hair.

But as she looked in the mirror, a wave of dizziness swept over her. She clutched the edge of the counter, fighting a sudden onslaught of nausea. Then she sank slowly to her knees, too dizzy and sick to move. She pressed her head to the side of the cabinet and closed her eyes. She had had food poisoning once before, years ago. Had it felt like this? Her only real memory of that time was feeling sicker than she ever had before.

Chapter Fourteen

Lucas paused at the bottom of the steps to brush a hand through his hair. The knowledge that Anna hadn't hesitated to accept his invitation encouraged him. He was sure she was attracted to him, but he worried her lingering feelings for her late husband would prevent her from acting on that attraction. He knew only one way to find out. He mounted the steps and rang the doorbell.

Inside, Jacquie barked and he heard the click of her toenails on the hardwood floor as she raced to the door. She pressed her nose to the window to the left of the door and barked again. Lucas smiled, anticipating Anna's greeting.

But the door remained shut and no footsteps moved toward it. Jacquie barked again and Lucas pressed the button for the doorbell. The chimes sounded clearly, but even if they hadn't, Anna couldn't have missed Jacquie's increasingly frantic clamor.

He knocked. "Anna! It's Lucas! Is everything okay?"

Maybe she was in the shower. He checked the

time. Six thirty-five. He took out his phone and dialed Anna's number. The phone rang and rang then went to voice mail. He ended the call and tried the doorknob. Locked. Could he break it down?

Before he could decide, the door eased open. Anna, gray-faced and bleary-eyed, sagged against the doorframe. Jacquie ceased barking and came to press against her mistress, face full of concern.

"Lucas, I'm so sorry," Anna said, her voice breathy and weak.

"What's happened?" he asked, alarmed. "You don't look well." Probably not the thing to say to a woman you wanted to date, but it was the truth. Anna looked ill.

"I don't know what's come over me." She covered her eyes with one hand. "I'm not feeling well."

She pushed herself away from the door frame and swayed. Lucas caught hold of her and steadied her. "I'm so sorry," she said again, then pulled back and staggered away.

He stepped into the house and followed her. He found her kneeling in front of the toilet in the hallway bathroom, being sick. "Oh, Anna," he said, and knelt behind her to hold back her hair. When she had finished retching, she sat up, one hand to her mouth.

"Lucas, this is terrible," she said.

He patted her shoulder, stood and wet a rag at the sink. He wiped her cheeks then gave it to her, left once more, and returned shortly with a glass of water. "Just sip this," he instructed, and handed it to her. Then he flushed the toilet, closed the lid, and sat on it, facing her. How many times had he done this for Jenny when she was sick from the chemotherapy?

"It must be food poisoning," Anna said. She pressed the washcloth to her cheek. "Gemma told me not to eat that chicken sandwich. I should have listened to her." Her eyes met his, watery with tears. "I'm sorry I won't be able to keep our date."

"That's okay." He looked into her eyes and noted that her pupils were slightly dilated. "Are you sure you're okay?" he asked. "Do you need to go to the hospital?"

"No!" She sat straighter, suddenly more alert. She gathered her legs under her as if to rise, and he stood to help her. "I'm already feeling better. I threw up once before you got here. Whatever it was, I think it's mostly out of my system now." She laid the washcloth on the edge of the sink and leaned forward to study her reflection. "Give me a minute and we'll talk."

He left the bathroom and waited in the hall while water ran. She emerged smelling of mint toothpaste, her hair combed, still pale, but the gray cast was gone. "Let's go in the living room," she said.

She didn't object when he put his arm around her and led her to the sofa. Her skin was warm but dry and she seemed steadier on her feet. He settled her on the sofa, then went into the kitchen and found crackers and flavored seltzer. "These may help," he said, bringing them to her.

"Thanks."

He sat beside her, Jacquie on her other side, while

she nibbled crackers and sipped the soda. "Before you got sick, how was your day going?" he asked.

"Good," she said. "We had some new shelves installed in the shop, something I've wanted since I opened the place. The guy who was just leaving when you arrived was the carpenter. He used to work for Jonas."

"The one who wants to buy the Dart."

"That's right." She set aside her glass and the crackers. "Would you like to see it?"

"I would," he said. "But it can wait until you're feeling better."

"I'm much better." She stood. "Let me show you."

He didn't detect any signs of weakness or dizziness as she moved through the kitchen to a door that led to the garage. She flipped on the light then moved to a tarp-covered vehicle on the far side of the space. He helped her fold back the tarp to reveal a red-and-Bondo-gray classic Dodge Dart, the insides gutted. "Jonas found it in a client's barn five years ago and bought it for a few hundred dollars." She smoothed her hand along the hood. "He spent a lot more than that restoring it, but I know he loved every minute of it. It's so sad he didn't get to finish it."

And she had kept the half-finished project in her garage all these months since Jonas's death. Because it reminded her of him? Because it made her feel closer to him? Probably all that and more.

She looked up at him. "I should have sold it a long time ago, but I don't know." She shrugged. "It almost felt like I was betraying him. Silly, I know. Do you have something like that from Jenny that you saved? Or do men not do that?"

His instinct was to look away, to brush off the question. But she deserved his honesty. "I don't have anything like that," he said. "But I didn't love Jenny the way you loved Jonas."

"What do you mean?"

He took her arm. "Let's go back inside and I'll tell you the story." Better they both be sitting down for this.

They settled onto the sofa and she sat back and studied him. "What's the story?" she asked.

He looked up at the ceiling, as if he might find the right words written there. "Once upon a time there was a man named Lucas who dated a woman he liked a lot. He loved her, but not enough to marry her. Not enough to make a commitment to stay with her forever. He thought she understood that, but after they moved in together, he realized she believed there would be more—a ring, a proposal, a ceremony, a happily-ever-after.

"He wanted to make her happy. To give her all the things she deserved, but in the end, he let her down. He couldn't commit to marriage. So she started packing her things and looking for an apartment, and they tried to part as friends. Then she started feeling sick and went to the doctor and found out she had cancer. They stayed together and he looked after her. But she never got the happy ending she wanted."

He rested his elbows on his knees and hunched forward, trying not to read rejection in the silence that stretched between them. Then her hand caressed his back. "Oh, Lucas," she said.

"Her sister hates me," he said. "She thought I should have married Jenny anyway, knowing she was dying."

"That's very unfair," Anna said.

He straightened and found the courage to look at her. Her expression was soft, sympathetic. "I was going to do it, too. I got a ring and proposed and everything. But Jenny was smart and she saw through me. She told me no, that we made better friends than lovers."

"You were a good friend to her," Anna said. "You stayed with her until the end. You loved her in a different way."

"I think she knew that, but I still felt like a terrible person," he said.

"Lucas, you didn't do anything wrong. It would have been dishonest to let her think otherwise."

"Maybe dishonest, but would it have been kinder?"

"Maybe, but you can't know that." She tucked her hair behind one ear and looked down at her lap. "I know in the last months Jonas was alive, the best thing I could do for him was to listen when he wanted to talk and to be a presence in the room when he was too weak to speak. You were those things for Jenny, I think."

"I still feel guilty."

"Welcome to the club." She sighed. "Guilt is a part of death, I think. No matter how much we do for our loved ones, there is always the thought that maybe we could have done more. What if I had insisted Jonas go to the doctor the first time he'd come home complaining of a back ache? But the man worked construction. Aches and pains were part of the job."

"So how do you deal with the guilt?"

"Maybe I hang on to a car he loved, even though I never liked it all that much." Anna's smile surprised her, almost as much as the realization that she could now see the humor in such a sad situation.

"Maybe now you're ready to move on," he said.

She leaned closer to him and slid one hand across his back to rest at his waist. It was an intimate touch; one that made her aware of the heat building within her. A longing for things she had thought out of reach. "How do you know when you're ready to move on, to take the next step?" she asked.

He angled toward her, his eyes locked to hers. "I think you have to simply move and see where your steps take you."

She slid her hand up his back to cup his head and lifted her lips to his. He stilled, his mouth against hers, caught and held. He made a sound in the back of his throat like a groan and nudged against her. His mouth moved, and his hands, gathering her close and pressing her against him.

A flood of sensation—relief, exhilaration and desire—rocketed through her. She caressed the nape of his neck, warm and silky, the ends of his close-cropped hair tickling the backs of her fingers, and slanted her mouth to his, wanting to explore every sensitive millimeter of him.

And she wanted to be closer. She rose up to strad-
dle him. He was hard, his erection pressed against
her. The sensation made her feel hot and lit up inside, sparks at every erogenous zone. She kissed him
more passionately still, eyes closed on the edge of
complete abandon.

Then he pushed her away, just enough that he
could look at her. "Are you okay with this?" he asked.
"If you're still feeling unwell, we can wait."

"I feel great," she said. "Fully recovered, I promise." She had never shaken off a case of food poisoning this quickly, but maybe sex—or at least
arousal—had health benefits she didn't know about.
She leaned in to plant a soft kiss on his jaw. "I want
this," she said. "I've wanted it for a while now."

"I want it, too." She thought he would kiss her
again, but instead he continued to look at her, his
hands at her waist, still holding her a little apart from
him. "You are so beautiful," he said.

Another side effect of desire, she thought, since
her hair was uncombed, her face bare of makeup and
probably too pale. But he made her feel beautiful, and
that counted for a lot. It helped make her less nervous,
and his own honesty with her made her want to return
the favor. "I'm a little nervous," she said. "We might
need to take it slow." She trailed one hand down his
chest, unable to look him in the eye. Doing so would
make her forget what she needed to say. "Don't feel
bad if I cry a little. I'm a pretty emotional person."

"We'll take it as slow as you need," he said, and
started with a long, slow kiss.

Eventually, she led him to the bedroom, where they undressed, also slowly, and the sight of him, naked, made her heart race. Then she registered the adoring way he was looking at her and felt a little dizzy, but in a good way. She sat on the bed and took his hand, intending to pull him down. He hesitated, and pain flickered through his eyes.

"What is it?" she asked.

He shook his head. "It's nothing."

She considered how she might have felt if they had been in his apartment, in his bedroom. "Don't worry," she said. "I redid this room last summer. This is a brand-new bed."

He looked sheepish, but also relieved. "It wouldn't have mattered," he said.

"It matters to me." She hadn't purchased the bed with the idea of making love to another man in it; she had wanted to spend the night not sharing space with all the memories of her and Jonas together. Now she could make new memories with Lucas.

They lay facing each other, studying one another like explorers mapping new territory. He discovered the scar on her shin from a bad fall in rocky terrain while training Jacquie, and she smiled at the almost perfectly heart-shaped birthmark on his hip. And then looking and touching turned to tasting and stroking. "Do you like this?" he asked. "How about this?"

"What if we do this?" she suggested, and so they negotiated their passion.

Her body woke as if from a long sleep and every

sensation felt new. She arched against him and cried out with pleasure, and couldn't seem to stop smiling. By the time he rolled on a condom and positioned himself against her, she welcomed him eagerly.

I still remember how to do this, she thought as they began to move together. She closed her eyes and surrendered to the flood of emotions, letting the wonderful tension build, moving toward release.

In the end, she didn't cry, but he did. Silent tears clung to his lashes as he leaned forward to kiss her as they clung together, sated. "I didn't know I could be this happy again," he said.

"I know." She kissed his eyes, tasting the salt. The worst thing in the world had happened to them both but they could still find joy. It was a kind of miracle, one that deserved both his tears and the smile she couldn't erase from her lips.

ANNA WOKE THE next morning to the sound of the shower running. She looked beside her in bed, at the rumpled sheets and the imprint of Lucas's head still on the pillow, and a warm thrill spread through her. She hugged herself, scarcely daring to believe how happy she was.

The bathroom door opened and Lucas emerged, towel around his hips, the muscles of his arms and shoulders bunching as he rubbed a second towel over his hair.

Anna sat up, pulling the sheet around her. "Good morning."

"Good morning." He smiled and moved to the side of the bed to kiss her. "How are you feeling?"

"I'm feeling great." A little tired, a little sore, and not ready to face a huge meal, but considering how sick she had been when he'd first arrived, she felt fantastic. "I think I'm fully recovered."

"That's good," he said. "I didn't want to wake you, but I have to be at work early today."

"That's okay," she said. "I have training at Search and Rescue headquarters this morning." She reached for her robe and slid into it, aware of him watching her.

Before she could cinch it closed, he moved to put his hands around her waist and pull her close. "I really do hate to leave," he said, nuzzling her neck.

"Mmm." She pressed against him then forced herself to pull away. "You're very tempting, but we'd both better get dressed."

He sighed. "You're right." He picked up the clothes he had worn last night from the chair by the bed and began to dress. She indulged herself in openly admiring him. This was a picture that would carry her through even the most boring training class.

Only when he was buckling his belt did she move into the bathroom to get ready herself.

When she emerged ten minutes later, he was waiting with a cup of coffee. "I can't stay to eat," he said. "I need to get home and change into my uniform."

"Maybe I'll see you after your shift," she said.

"Maybe. What are you training for today?"

"Wilderness first-aid triage. There's a lecture, then

some practical exercises." She took Jacquie's leash from a hook by the back door and the dog danced over to her. "I need to walk her before I head to the class. She's not going to be happy about being left behind. When I put on my Search and Rescue jacket, she thinks she's going to work."

"Poor abandoned baby," he said, and rubbed the dog's ears. Jacquie leaned against his leg, momentarily forgetting about her walk.

They said goodbye and Anna walked Jacquie along their usual route to the town park, around the track twice, then back home. She fed the dog, made sure she had plenty of water, and slipped out the door while Jacquie was still eating.

All of the rookies and most of the veteran Search and Rescue volunteers gathered at SAR headquarters, a large concrete-floored building with roll-up metal doors that housed all the search and rescue equipment and provided meeting space for the group. Anna sat with fellow rookies Grace Wilcox, Nancy Phillips and Caleb Edmond.

Chris Mercer soon joined them. The blue-haired artist wasn't a rookie, but she had been away from SAR for a year while she'd served as artist-in-residence at Rocky Mountain National Park. "I've taken this class before," she said as she settled onto the folding chair next to Anna. "But it's been a few years. I figured it would be a good idea to refresh my memory."

Nurse Danny Irwin, a veteran volunteer, was teaching the class, assisted by Hannah Richards, an Eagle Mountain paramedic and current medical officer for the group. Anna forced herself to focus on the slide presentation that began the class, outlining the most common injuries they might encounter during backcountry rescues.

But when the course shifted to a lecture on identifying, assessing and treating a lengthy list of possible injuries, her mind kept drifting to last night and her wonderful encounter with Lucas. The evening had been so much better than her fantasies. She had thought she would be nervous, but they had been so into each other, she really hadn't had an opportunity to overthink what was happening.

"Let's take a break and, when we come back, we'll go through some mock exercises," Danny finally announced.

Anna and Nancy headed to the ladies' room then joined the others at a table set with coffee and tea, doughnuts and fruit. Anna was pouring hot water over a tea bag when phones began going off all over the room, including her own.

"Somebody is lucky today," Ryan Welch said as he looked at his phone. "We've got a callout and everyone is already right here."

Sheri was already on the phone with the 9-1-1 dispatcher. "A helitracks chopper spotted someone in a vehicle stuck up on Black Eagle pass," she said.

"That road is still closed, isn't it?" Danny asked. "There's still a ton of snow up there."

"It is," Tony Meisner confirmed. "This person either didn't know that, or thought he could get through."

"It happens every few years," Ryan said. "People

look on a map and see the shortest route to their des-
tination is on a road that they don't realize is four-
wheel-drive only or open only seasonally."

"Ten years ago a couple froze to death when their
minivan got stuck and they tried to hike out," Sheri
said. "This guy is lucky the helicopter pilot spotted
him." She surveyed the group. "We'll take the Beast
and a couple of four-wheel-drive vehicles, but we'll
probably have to stop at some point and snowshoe
in. We don't know how long the driver has been up
there. The chopper pilot said he only saw one person, but it's always possible there were passengers
in the vehicle, so let's be prepared."

Within ten minutes, Anna was in Grace's Jeep
alongside Chris and Nancy, following the Beast,
a specially equipped Search and Rescue Jeep, up
Dixon Pass, toward the turnoff to the backcountry
road over Black Eagle pass.

"We're following a vehicle's tracks," Tony radioed
shortly after the SAR caravan turned onto the Jeep
road. Ten minutes later, everyone was forced to stop.

Anna piled out of the vehicle with the others and
Sheri walked back to them. "There's a little snowslide blocking the road," Sheri said. "We'll have to
snowshoe from here."

Everyone donned snowshoes and slipped on packs
and began the climb up the road. "The helicopter pilot
said he spotted the stranded motorist almost to the
summit of the pass," Sheri said.

"How did he make it all the way up there?" Nancy
asked.

"After you pass the Homestead Mine, it's too narrow to turn around," Tony said. "He probably just kept going forward until he couldn't move anymore. There's no phone service up here, and no one else was going to come along. If he didn't have snowshoes, hiking down was going to be pretty grueling. The snow's at least four feet deep."

Even snowshoeing was pretty strenuous. Before long, they were all unzipping jackets and stripping off hats. Anna marched along behind Grace, legs already aching, but she wasn't going to complain. This was what rescue work was—lots of hard work on behalf of a stranger.

Another half hour passed and a shout rose up from the head of the line, the message passed back to Anna and the other rookies in the rear of the column. "They've spotted the car," Grace told Anna.

Moments later, they were gathered around a very cold and very grateful young man. Darryl Singh's teeth chattered as he thanked them and accepted blankets and hot packs, and hot chocolate from a thermos. "I was trying to get to Eagle Mountain," he said. "I've never been here before and the map said this was the shortest way." He looked around him, at the snow piled higher than his head on three sides, the nose of his small sedan buried in a wall of snow. "I'm from Florida," he said. "I've never seen so much snow in my life."

"Who were you going to see in Eagle Mountain?" Sheri asked.

He shook his head. "Oh, that doesn't matter."

"If someone is expecting you, they're probably worried," Carrie said. "We can radio and let them know you're all right."

"I was just making a delivery, as a favor for a friend," he said.

"Who was the delivery for?" Sheri pressed.

"A bakery."

"Do you mean Weiss Bakery?" Anna asked.

"Yes, that's it." Singh looked pained. "I don't even know what the package is. I'm just doing it as a favor. And to earn extra money." He looked back at his car, expression mournful. "How much is it going to cost me to get back down from here?"

"We'll take you to town for free," Danny said. "But you'll have to hire a wrecker to come up and get your car. And it won't be cheap."

Singh looked as if he wanted to cry.

"How long have you been up here?" Tony asked.

Singh pushed back the blanket to check his watch. "Five hours. I was wondering how long it would take to freeze to death."

"You're lucky a helicopter pilot spotted you and notified us," Sheri said.

He nodded, expression still sorrowful. "Yes. I am very lucky."

They had brought extra snowshoes, and fitted Singh with a pair and started back down the road with him in the middle of the group. They had traveled halfway back to their vehicles when he let out a wail. "The package!" he cried. "I forgot the package for the bakery!"

"Leave it," Tony said. "You can get it later when they retrieve your car. It's not worth risking hypothermia to get it back."

He looked as if he wanted to protest, but Tony slung an arm around his shoulder. "Come on," he said. "You really do need to get somewhere warmer."

Back at the cars, they settled Singh into the Beast. "We'll take you to the sheriff's office and they'll help you arrange to take care of your vehicle and get you back home," Sheri said. "How are you feeling?"

"Very upset," he said. "But warmer."

"Warm is good," she said.

The caravan started back down the mountain. "I don't think that guy knows how lucky he is," Grace said as she piloted her Jeep through the icy ruts in the Beast's wake. "He didn't have any kind of emergency gear in his car and he wasn't dressed for the weather. He was wearing tennis shoes and didn't even have a winter coat."

"He thought he was making a quick trip to Eagle Mountain," Chris said.

"I wonder what he was delivering to the bakery," Anna said.

"I guess some kind of specialty ingredient or something," Nancy said.

Back at SAR headquarters, everyone pitched in to clean up the materials from the training class. Sheri and Tony drove Darryl Singh to the sheriff's department and everyone else left for home or work or wherever they needed to be.

Anna started home but detoured to the bakery instead. She found Sandy decorating cupcakes, each chocolate-frosted cake topped with a pink or blue rosebud. "These are for a baby shower tomorrow," Sandy said. "As soon as I finish them, I'm closing for the day."

"Do you know Darryl Singh?" Anna asked.

Sandy shook her head. "Never heard of him."

"I just came from a search and rescue call." Anna settled onto a stool beside Sandy's worktable. "He was stuck up on Black Eagle pass. He saw the route on the map and thought it was a shortcut to Eagle Mountain."

Sandy snorted. "I guess he's not from around here?"

"He said he was from Florida."

"He's lucky he didn't freeze to death up there."

"He said he was on his way to Eagle Mountain to deliver something to you."

Sandy stilled. "What was he delivering to me?"

"He didn't say. He just said a friend had paid him to drive the package over to you."

"Where is the package now?"

"He left it back in his car. Do you know what it is?"

Sandy shook her head and went back to adding icing rosebuds to the top of the cupcakes. "No idea. Maybe it was something Dave ordered before he died."

"Do you get deliveries like that very often?" Anna asked.

"We get supplies from all over the place," Sandy said. "Whoever can give us the best price. That's how a small business has to operate to make a profit."

"It just seemed odd to have a guy like that driving something here personally on a Saturday morning."

Sandy laid aside the icing bag and faced Anna. "Why are you so interested? What do you care where we get our supplies?"

"It just struck me as odd," Anna said, determined not to let Sandy cow her.

"It isn't odd. There are lots of specialty suppliers in food services." Sandy picked up the icing bag. "These bags come from a place in Denmark. They gave us the best deal, so that's who we bought from. If somebody in Junction or Denver or Timbuktu has what we need at a good price, we're going to buy from them. Not everything has to come from one big wholesaler, you know."

Anna nodded. "Okay. Well, whatever it is, I hope you don't need it right away. Until Mr. Singh gets his car hauled down, your package is stuck up on Black Eagle pass."

"I'll manage." Sandy picked up the tray of cupcakes, carried it to a glassed-in cooler, and slid it inside.

"Thanks again for the cupcakes you sent home with me," Anna said, hoping to thaw some of the frost that had chilled Sandy's attitude. "They were delicious, as always."

Sandy frowned at her. "So you ate the cupcakes? Both of them?"

"I did. I had the second one yesterday afternoon." She grimaced. "I guess it was kind of wasted, though." She rubbed her stomach. "I made the mistake of eating a sandwich for lunch that had been in the refrigerator at my shop for more than a few days. Not long after I ate that cupcake, I was sick as could be. Food poisoning."

"How are you feeling now?" Sandy asked.

"Much better. I threw up a couple of times and I guess I got it all out of my system." She shook her head. "I'll be a little pickier about what I eat from now on," she said. "Jonas always teased me about my sensitive stomach. He could eat all kinds of things, but if something is the least off, I can't handle it."

"I need to close up now." Sandy walked to the door and turned the sign to Closed.

"I'll leave you to it," Anna said. "I just wanted to let you know about that package."

"Forget about the package," Sandy said. "I'm sure it's nothing important."

Anna left and drove home.

Sandy had always been a hard person to read, but lately she confused Anna even more. One moment she was asking Anna for help and giving her cupcakes, the next she was ticked off that Anna had stopped by. A lot of people might have written her off, but Anna remembered how grief had played with her own emotions. She had cycled from anger to despair in the blink of an eye, and had probably annoyed more than one person who'd tried to help her. She didn't want to abandon Sandy to go through that storm alone. For now, at least, she would continue to check on her and try to help her, if not for Sandy's sake, then for Dave. He had loved her and he would appreciate that Anna was trying to be there for her.

THAT AFTERNOON, Anna stood on the side of the driveway and watched as Bobby winched the Dart onto his trailer. Bobby's wife, Melody, eight months pregnant, stood beside her. "Bobby is so excited about getting this car," Melody said. "Though I don't know when he's going to have time to work on it, between the business and the new baby." She rubbed the swell of her abdomen and smiled.

"Jonas would be glad to know it's going to someone who will love it as much as he did," Anna said.

Melody's smile faded. "This must be hard for you," she said.

"Not as hard as I thought it would be, really." Anna turned to Melody. "I guess that's a good sign that it's time to let go."

"We would have been happy to pay you for the Dart," Melody said. "I'm sure it's worth a lot of money."

"It's worth more to me knowing it's going to you. I'm sure that's what Jonas would have wanted."

Bobby moved around the trailer to join them. "All set," he said. His grin made him look very young. "Thanks again."

"Thank you for giving it a good home." Anna moved toward him to shake hands, but he wrapped his arms around her and pulled her close in a hug. "Don't be a stranger," he said.

"I won't."

She watched them go, then closed the garage door

and went inside the house. She felt lighter. Not happy, exactly, but not as sad, either. She really was letting go.

Moving on. She took out her phone.

I just gave away the Dart to Bobby Fitch.

Lucas's reply came quickly.

How are you feeling?

Good. It was time.

Good.

Want to come over tonight?

I'd like that.

She hesitated, hand hovering over the screen. Bring a toothbrush, she typed. She intended for him to stay with her all night.

HOURS LATER, after dinner and an evening of leisurely lovemaking, the tinny chimes of his ringtone pulled Lucas from sleep—the kind of sleep where waking feels like surfacing from deep under water. By the time he struggled to open his eyes, Anna was sitting up in bed beside him, the blanket pulled to her shoulders, staring at the phone that vibrated and buzzed on the bedside table. He grabbed the phone and swiped to answer the call. "Hello?"

"Deputy Malone, this is Shaylin Brown. I'm sorry to wake you so early on a Sunday, but I'm worried about George."

Lucas shifted his gaze to the clock on the bedside table. Six fourteen glowed in red numerals. Not the middle of the night, but early for a call from someone who was practically a stranger. "What about George?" he asked.

"He didn't come home last night." Shaylin's voice was ragged, as if she had been shouting, or crying. "I keep calling his cell phone and I don't get an answer. He's not at the office. None of his friends or best clients have heard from him."

"Have you contacted the Junction police?" Lucas asked, becoming more awake by the moment.

"I did. They told me I can file a missing person's report, but they said a grown man failing to come home isn't that unusual. But it is. George is always home by nine. Usually earlier."

"Do you and Mr. Anton live together?" Lucas asked.

"Yes. And he always comes home. He calls if he's going to be late."

Lucas ran a hand through his hair. "When was the last time you saw him or spoke to him?" he asked.

"At the office yesterday afternoon. He said he was driving to Eagle Mountain later that evening to see Sandy Weiss. He said he'd meet me at the house, and not to worry if he was late. But he never came home at all. He doesn't answer his phone. I tried contacting Mrs. Weiss, but she's not answering, either."

Lucas could have told Shaylin that this wasn't really his jurisdiction or his case, but the connection to Sandy Weiss interested him. "Was it usual for George to meet with clients that late in the day, especially on a weekend?" he asked.

"He meets with them when people are available," she said. "He often meets with restaurant owners in the evening, but sometimes with suppliers, too."

"Did George indicate there was anything unusual about this meeting with Mrs. Weiss?" he asked. "Was he fearful of any kind of trouble?"

"He was going to ask her about the things you had told him about her wanting to close the business and stop paying on the loan he had made to Dave. He said he wanted to work something out with her."

"Was George angry about that?" Lucas asked.

"No. That wasn't George. He wants to help people. He wants to make a living while he does so, but he loves putting people together who can help each other. He loves his work. But after what happened with Dave Weiss, I'm scared. What if whoever hurt Dave goes after George?" Her voice broke.

"I want you to be honest with me, Shaylin," he said. "Was George involved in any way with dealing drugs?"

"Absolutely not!" Her voice rose and she talked faster, even more agitated. "George heard there was a group of people selling drugs out of restaurants. He knew some people who got arrested, and the local cops questioned him about it more than once. But he didn't have anything to do with it, and he swore he would turn in anyone he found out was involved. He had a younger sister who died of an overdose when she was twenty-two and he's been absolutely set against drugs since then."

It was a good story, but was it true? Michaela had told him the Junction cops were watching George Anton and hadn't found any evidence against him, but he wouldn't be the first dealer to outsmart the police. "I want you to call the Junction sheriff's department and ask to speak to Del Alvarez," he said. "You tell him your story, and that I sent you. He'll help you."

"I'll do that, but will you at least look for George in Eagle Mountain?"

"I'll drive over to the Weisses' place and ask Sandy if she's heard from George," Lucas said.

"Please call me as soon as you hear anything," she said. "I've been up all night worrying."

"I will." He ended the call and turned to look at Anna, who was still sitting up in bed, watching him. "George Anton is missing," he said. "He was supposed to be on his way to Eagle Mountain to meet with Sandy Weiss yesterday evening and he hasn't been heard from since."

"You need to talk to Sandy," she said.

"Yeah." He glanced at the clock. "And the sooner, the better."

"I'll make coffee." She pushed back the covers and he had a tantalizing glimpse of her, naked, before she pulled on her robe. He would have liked nothing better than to pull her back into bed and spend the

day making love to her. But Shailyn's barely sup-
pressed panic over George's whereabouts cooled his
desire. He still had little proof that Dave Weiss hadn't
committed suicide, but too many things associated
with the Weiss Bakery didn't make sense. He and
the rest of the sheriff's department were always one
step behind everyone involved in this case, from the
anonymous note-writer to the person who had shat-
tered the window of the bakery. Maybe this was his
chance to get one step ahead for a change.

Chapter Fifteen

Anna set coffee to brew and returned to the bedroom to watch Lucas dress. She wasn't going to get tired of watching him do anything for a long while, she decided. She still tingled with the memory of their lovemaking last night. Why had she waited so long? "Let me call Sandy," she said. "She's more likely to answer a call from me at this hour, I would think."

"That's a good idea." He threaded his belt through the loops of his slacks and fastened the buckle. "Don't say anything about George. Just tell her I need to stop by and talk to her."

"All right." She pulled out her phone and found the number for Sandy and Dave's home. The number was still tagged as "Dave-Home." She hit the button to dial and waited while the phone rang and rang. Then it fell silent, not even going to voice mail. Next, she tried Sandy's cell phone. This time she received the message that said, "You have reached a number that is no longer in service."

"That's so odd," she said. "The number is programmed into my phone, so I know it's right." She punched in the number for the bakery. It rang and rang. "No one's answering at the bakery, either."

"Maybe she's busy with something and can't get to the phone." He finished putting on his shoes and straightened. "I'll try the bakery and, if she's not there, I'll check her house," he said.

Anna relaxed. "Of course. She's probably just swamped with customers." People wanted fresh pastries for breakfast, especially on a weekend morning.

Lucas moved to her and pulled her into his arms. "I'm sorry to have to leave like this."

"I understand." She snuggled closer. "Maybe you can come back tonight."

"I'd like that." He kissed her. A long, deep kiss she was sure was guaranteed to keep them both thinking about it all day. She wanted to cling to him but she didn't. They both had lives to live and work to do.

When he was gone, she dressed and drank a cup of coffee, then slipped a harness on Jacquie. Her usual routine was to walk the dog, then return to the house for breakfast before she settled in to read or garden or catch up on chores. Sunday was the only day Yarn and More wasn't open.

She and Jacquie often headed toward the dog park by the river, or the trail near the school. But this morning, she took a different route; one that would take her past Sandy and Dave's house. She didn't expect Sandy to be there, but it wouldn't hurt to check, would it? She hadn't heard all of the call from Shaylin Brown, but Lucas's side of the conversation had sounded serious. So many strange things had been happening to Sandy since Dave's death. Shaylin had telephoned because she was concerned about George Anton, but Anna wondered if Sandy wasn't the one who was really in danger.

A chill hung heavy in the air as Jacquie and Anna walked briskly toward the Weisses'. Lights glowed in most of the houses they passed, and she waved to the few people she saw. Jacquie sniffed around the garbage cans awaiting pickup at the curb, and barked at a gray squirrel that raced across the street in front of her. Anna pulled her coat more tightly around her and breathed in deeply the cold, crisp air. If not for her worries about her friend, this would have been an enjoyable walk; a reminder that she should vary her route more often.

Lights glowed in the front rooms of Sandy's home, too, and her Jeep sat in the driveway. Anna climbed the steps to the door and rang the bell while Jacquie sat at her side and stared at the door. After a long moment, the door opened and Sandy peered out. "Anna, what are you doing here?" she asked.

"Jacquie and I were out for a walk and I saw your light," Anna said. "I figured you'd be at the bakery at this hour, so I stopped to see if everything was okay."

"I had to close the bakery for a few days," Sandy said. "Until the window can be replaced."

Anna nodded. How much should she say about Lucas and George Anton? She thrust her hand in the pocket of her coat. "It's cold this morning," she said. "Could I talk you out of a cup of coffee?"

Sandy frowned, and Anna was sure she was going

to make some excuse, but she opened the door a little wider. "Sure. You can keep me company while I pack."

Anna and Jacquie followed Sandy through the darkened living room, but even in the dim light, Anna couldn't help notice the room was almost empty. "What happened to your furniture?" she asked.

"I sold it." She headed for the bedroom, and Anna rushed to keep up. A suitcase lay open on the unmade bed, clothes piled around it. "Where are you going?" Anna asked.

"Since I have to close the bakery anyway, I thought it would be nice to get away for a few days." She picked up a stack of folded shirts and fitted them into the suitcase. "It's been a little tense. I thought maybe a trip would help me relax."

"That's a wonderful idea," Anna said. "Where will you go?"

"Someplace warm, I think." Sandy added a stack of shorts to the suitcase. "I'm tired of cold."

"Do you need me to do anything while you're gone?" Anna asked. "Water the plants or collect the mail?" Sandy didn't have pets that would need care.

"I've got that all taken care of." Sandy fitted a pair of sandals in the side of the case.

"I tried calling you this morning," Anna said. "But I got a message your phone was disconnected."

"Why were you calling me?" Sandy continued to fit items into the suitcase.

"George Anton is missing," Anna said. "I was wondering if you had heard from him lately."

Sandy turned and stared, as if Anna had grown an extra head. "Why would I know anything about George?"

"His assistant said he had a meeting with you yesterday afternoon, here in Eagle Mountain."

Sandy shook her head. "I don't know anything about that."

You're lying, Anna thought. "I always wondered if he was the person who threatened you," she said.

Sandy turned back to the suitcase. "I never did get you that coffee," she said. "There's some in the kitchen. Why don't you fix us both a cup while I finish up here?"

"Sure." Anna left the room, more certain than ever that Sandy was hiding something. But was it something important, or just Sandy's usual instinct to resist any attempts by Anna to get closer? Jacquie trotted after her, probably hoping for her usual after-walk biscuit. Anna found mugs and filled them from the coffee machine by the sink. Did Sandy take cream or sugar? She couldn't remember. She moved to the doorway. "Sandy, how do you want your coffee?" she called.

"Black is fine," came the answer.

Anna added creamer from a carton in the refrigerator to her own cup and then carried both mugs back toward the bedroom.

She only got as far as the living room. Sandy met her there, a gun in her hand. "You can set the coffee down," she said. "No sense spilling it on the carpet."

Anna stared at the gun, which Sandy held pointed at her. "What are you doing?" she asked.

"The problem with you, Anna, is that you don't know how to take a hint."

THE BAKERY WAS shut tight when Lucas arrived. The large front window was boarded up and a hand-lettered sign on the front door said Closed for Repairs. No cars sat in the lot. Lucas made a wide circle and parked with his SUV facing the road, then got out and walked around the building. Nothing looked disturbed. He took out his phone, looked up the number for the Weiss home and dialed it. It rang and rang, but no one answered, and eventually it fell silent once more.

He stopped at the back of the building, at a pair of metal double doors that apparently led into a massive freezer. When this had been a meat market, this freezer would have held meat that would be carried through these doors and loaded onto trucks. Ashley Dietrich had said the Weisses stored flour and other ingredients here. He reached up and tried the door, but it was locked by a heavy hasp and padlock.

He turned away, but a thumping noise froze him in his tracks. The noise came again. He stared at the freezer doors then eased one hand to the butt of the pistol in the holster at his side. "Who's there?" he called.

The thumping continued. Not louder, but more rapid. Lucas approached the door. "Who's there?" he shouted.

A noise, almost, but not quite, like a voice. He pressed his ear to the freezer door and listened.

Help, he thought he heard, faint and muffled. *Somebody help.*

Chapter Sixteen

The sheriff arrived at Weiss Bakery shortly after 7:00 a.m., along with two deputies and a locksmith. The locksmith went to work right away, drilling out the lock, while Lucas and the others waited a short distance away. "Who do you think is in there?" the sheriff asked.

"Either Sandy Weiss or George Anton," Lucas said. "They're both missing."

Travis, hands on his hips, looked around them. "This would be a good place to receive or transport drugs or stolen goods," he said. "Lots of space. No neighbors."

"Are you thinking Dave Weiss was involved in something like that?" Lucas asked. "And that's why he was killed?"

"It's something to consider," Travis said.

"Got it," the locksmith called, and swung the hasp away from the door. Lucas and Deputy Dwight Prentice moved forward to tug at the door. Sunlight illuminated the interior of the freezer, where the still figure of George Anton lay on the floor, wrists bound behind his back, rope wrapped around his ankles. His eyes were closed, and frost clung to his skin.

"Call an ambulance," Lucas said, and dropped to his knees beside the man. He touched one icy cheek. "George!" he said. "George, can you hear me?"

"I TRIED TO do this the easy way," Sandy said, the gun still leveled at Anna. "The drugs I put in that cupcake should have made you go to sleep and never wake up."

"You poisoned the cupcakes you gave me?" Anna didn't quite believe what she was hearing. "That's why I was so sick?"

"Just one of the cupcakes," Sandy said. "I didn't want to take a chance on you eating the poisoned one first and the cops testing the other one. But, apparently, you've got an extra-sensitive stomach and you didn't keep the drugs down long enough for them to do their job."

"Why would you want to kill me?" Anna asked.

Sandy's mouth twisted into a sneer. "Why would anyone want to kill sweet, perfect Anna?" she mocked. "Maybe because you wouldn't stop asking questions. You were the one who spotted the ladder imprints and made the sheriff's department think that maybe Dave hadn't killed himself after all. And you were the one who sent the cops looking for George Anton, too. You kept questioning my story about being in debt, and that made your boyfriend, the cop, question it, too. I don't think you're smart enough to figure things out on your own, but you might stumble on the truth by sheer luck."

Anna's legs felt almost too weak to stand, but she was terrified that if she moved at all, Sandy would shoot her. She had to stay strong. To figure a way out of this. She had to keep Sandy talking. As long as they were talking, the other woman wasn't shooting. She latched onto the most alarming thing Sandy had said so far. "Do you mean Dave didn't commit suicide?"

"He was just like you, always asking questions. I thought he didn't pay any attention to the money side of things. He always said he was happy to leave me in charge of the finances. I would have bet half my savings that he never even looked at the books." Sandy waved the gun in the air, making Anna flinch. "Then one day he asked why we didn't have more money in the bank. And why was the payment to George Anton late? And why was I at the bakery when I had told him I was going out for a run? And who was the man I met there?" Her eyes blazed and her face reddened. "He had *followed* me. Can you believe that? And he had the nerve to accuse me of cheating on him."

"But you weren't cheating on him," Anna said. She glanced from Sandy's face, so angry, to the gun in her hand. Sandy seemed distracted, remembering this interaction with Dave. Could Anna use that distraction to her advantage?

"Of course not. I wouldn't do that. Everything I did was for us! To secure our future, so we wouldn't have to work so hard."

"What were you doing?" Anna asked.

"Why is everyone so nosy?" Sandy waved the gun again. Anna worried it would fire accidentally. She wanted to ask Sandy to stay still, but guessed anything she said at this point was likely to upset her more. So she stayed silent, hoping Sandy would keep talking.

"I told Dave I was being careful. And it was so easy. Just bake a dozen cupcakes, hollow out the centers and put a packet of drugs in each. Mark the cupcakes with a special design on the top and ship them off to restaurants, where the right people would spot the design, remove the packets of drugs and fill in the gap with chocolate. And who suspects cupcakes?" She laughed, and Anna shivered. There was nothing cheerful in the sound.

She cleared her throat. "So you were smuggling drugs in the cupcakes. Where did you get the drugs?" she asked.

"Why would I tell you?" Sandy asked. "Even if you aren't going to be around to talk."

"Dave found out?" Anna hastened to add. Anything to get Sandy to focus on something else. "And you had to get rid of him?"

"He insisted on double-checking the next shipment of baked goods and found the cupcakes with the extra 'surprise.' He went ballistic. A full-blown screaming fit. The whole time we were married, he never raised his voice to me, but he actually *threw* the box of cupcakes at me. He insisted we go to the sheriff and tell him everything. I told him that was the fastest way to get us both killed, but he wouldn't listen."

"What did you do?" Anna asked. She kept her voice quiet, as if making casual conversation. She wanted Sandy to say that the drug dealer had murdered Dave. That the dealer was the one who had threatened Sandy and shot out the window of the bakery. But part of her already knew that wasn't right.

"I suggested we go for a drive to calm down and talk things out," she said. "I made coffee to take with us, and a couple of bear claws to go with the coffee. A little picnic. But I put a big dose of that dog tranquilizer in his coffee. He didn't even notice, but it calmed him down enough that I could deal with him."

"Where did you get dog tranquilizers?" Anna had told herself she was going to be quiet, but she couldn't keep back the question.

Sandy looked smug. "I lied to the cops. Dave did have a dog, years ago. Before we married. Bruno had seizures, so Dave had to give him phenobarbital. The dog died while we were still dating, but Dave never threw anything away. I was cleaning out a cabinet after I moved in and found them, but I decided to hang on to them. You never know when something like that will come in handy."

Anna tried to hide her revulsion. "But the medication didn't kill Dave," she said.

"I told you, I wasn't trying to kill him. Not with that. I wanted people to think he'd killed himself, so I had him drive out to Panther Point. I thought about pushing him off a cliff and telling people he had jumped, but decided it would be better if people thought I wasn't anywhere near him when it happened. So I decided to hang him."

Anna swallowed down a wave of nausea. "I saw the scene," she said. "How did you ever get him up in that tree?"

"He was all doped up. I walked him way back there to that cottonwood and we had our little picnic, then I suggested he lie down and take a nap. I went back to the truck and got the ladder and some rope. I set everything up, then coaxed him up the ladder. He was so out of it he didn't protest, but that also meant I had to do most of the heavy lifting." She laughed again. "Good thing I had all that practice carrying dead weight in firefighter training. I got the noose around his neck and the other end of the rope secured around the tree. Then all I had to do was pull the ladder away." She paused and studied Anna. "Don't look so horrified. He didn't suffer. He died within seconds."

Anna swallowed. "What happened to the ladder?" she asked.

"I drove farther into the mountains and dropped it down a mine shaft," she said. "Then I drove back to the place where the truck was found and left it there and walked home. I hid when any cars came by, but there wasn't much traffic, so I didn't have much trouble. I cleaned up the cupcakes, baked a new batch for the drugs, and played the part of a worried wife."

"What about the threatening notes?" Anna asked. "And the person who shot out the window of the bakery?"

Sandy smiled. "That was all me. I figured it wouldn't hurt if the sheriff thought I was in danger, too. And it was the perfect excuse for me to take the money I'd saved up and disappear. I let my supplier know what was going on and he agreed that was a good idea. We parted on good terms and he said he'd be happy to work with me again any time."

"Was it George Anton?" Anna asked.

"Everyone is going to think that, aren't they?" Sandy asked. "That was another great thing about this whole setup. George is the perfect suspect. Of course, I can't take credit for that. My supplier made sure the cops would focus on George. But good old George was just a patsy. He transported the drugs from me to the various pickup points at restaurants, and people there distributed the dope on the streets. George had no idea."

"Surely, he would have figured it out eventually," Anna said.

"Maybe." Sandy shrugged. "It doesn't matter now anyway." She steadied the gun again. "Now, I just have to take care of you and I can leave."

Chapter Seventeen

George groaned and his eyelids flickered. Lucas felt for a pulse and located a weak flutter. Even here, in the open doorway, he could feel the frosty chill of the freezer. Had George been in there all night? How had he not died? "Let's move him into the sun, where it's warmer," he said. He took off his coat and draped it over George's still figure. The sheriff and Dwight did the same, then they carried him to a spot on the loading dock in full sun.

The sheriff went into the freezer and emerged shortly, shaking his head. "We'll want to take a closer look, but I don't see anything incriminating in there."

The wail of an ambulance siren grew louder, and Dwight went around front to meet it. Lucas looked down at the still, unconscious man. "Who do you think put him in that freezer?" he asked.

"Whoever it was, what have they done with Sandy?" Travis asked.

The siren quieted and two paramedics raced around the side of the building. "What's the situation?" Hannah Richards asked.

"He was locked in a deep freeze," Travis said. "We don't know how long."

Hannah and EMT Emmet Baxter set to work, checking vital signs and placing warming packs around George's body. Hannah started an IV and began a saline drip. "The saline will help warm him, too," she explained. "There's a little frostbite on his bare fingers, but right now it doesn't look like he'll lose any digits."

George groaned again, more loudly, and turned his head from side to side.

Lucas knelt beside him. "George!" he called.

George opened his eyes and stared up at him. "You're going to be okay," Lucas said. "But we need to know what happened to Sandy."

George shook his head. "No," he said. "No, no, no."

Lucas gripped his shoulder. "You're going to be okay. But where is Sandy? We need to find her."

"Don't…know." George forced out the words. "She…did…this."

The sheriff joined Lucas next to George. "Are you saying Sandy did this to you?" he asked.

George nodded. "Tried…to…kill me."

"Why did Sandy try to kill you?" Lucas asked.

"I…found out…about…the drugs."

"What drugs?" Lucas asked. "What did you find out about the drugs?"

But George's eyes were closed and he didn't make an effort to speak again.

"We need to get him to the hospital," Hannah said.

Lucas and Travis both rose and stepped back.

"Do you think he's talking about the drugs that were being distributed by workers at the restaurants in Junction?" Lucas asked.

"Junction law enforcement suspected Anton was the source of the drugs," Travis said. "But maybe that wasn't the case." He looked up at the bakery. "Maybe they were coming from here."

"Those Surprise Cakes," Lucas said.

Travis nodded. "Maybe Weiss was baking more than party favors and chocolate into those cakes."

"Then why was he killed?" Lucas asked.

"Maybe he tried to double-cross his dealer."

"George said Sandy is the one who tried to kill him," Lucas said.

"We'd better find her," Travis said. "Let's check her house. Maybe we can figure out where she's headed."

Lucas pulled out his phone. "I'm going to call Anna," he said. "Just in case Sandy tries to get in touch with her."

"Tell her to stay away," Travis said.

He nodded and listened to the phone ring. And ring. "She's not answering," he said. His stomach tightened. Was she not answering because she was in the shower—or because Sandy had already gotten to her?

As SANDY LEVELED the gun, Anna turned to run. She wasn't going to stand there and be shot point-blank.

Jacquie whined and both women looked at the dog. "Jacquie, go!" Anna shouted.

But "go" wasn't a command in the dog's repertoire. Instead of leaving, she took a step toward Sandy, body tense, growling low. "Jacquie, no!" Anna shouted. Sandy had swiveled the gun at the dog. Anna tried to think of some command the dog would obey. Anything to get her out of harm's way.

"Jacquie, search!" she cried.

Jacquie looked to her, clearly confused. She hadn't been given a scent to focus in on. But she was also trained to do a more general search, the kind she might do after an avalanche or when searching for a body in a lake. "Search!" Anna said again, and pointed toward the kitchen.

She almost collapsed with relief when Jacquie turned and headed for the kitchen. But she had no time to savor the feeling as she turned to see that Sandy once more had the gun pointed at her. She forced herself to look in the other woman's eyes. There was nothing in Sandy's expression that she recognized as the woman Anna had once wanted to be friends with. All she saw was a chilling blankness.

"Sandy, don't do this," she pleaded.

"I'm actually going to enjoy this one," Sandy said. She slipped her finger into the trigger guard. Anna turned to run.

Jacquie barked, and her toenails scrabbled for purchase on the hardwood floor. The gun went off. Anna screamed and Sandy roared with rage.

Anna whirled around to see Sandy on the floor, trying to fight off Jacquie, who had her by the arm and refused to let go. The gun lay several feet away, half under the sofa. Anna crawled toward it and picked it up. Carefully. She had no idea how to shoot, but she knew enough to keep the weapon away from the woman who wanted to kill her.

"Stop! Police!" The door burst open and Lucas, followed by the sheriff and two other deputies, burst into the room. Anna let the gun fall from her hands and sagged against the sofa. There was more shouting, more barking, but she was only dimly aware of any of it.

"Are you all right?" Lucas knelt beside her, one arm around her shoulders.

She nodded and let herself lean against him. "I'm okay," she said.

"Could you call off Jacquie?" he asked.

She looked toward the dog, who stood over Sandy, her teeth still clamped around the other woman's wrist.

"Jacquie!" she called. "Jacquie, come!"

Jacquie released her hold on Sandy and trotted over. Anna let go of Lucas so she could hug the dog close.

"Good girl," she said. "Such a good girl."

Sandy swore and fought against the two deputies who put her in handcuffs and led her away. The sheriff came to stand beside Anna.

"What happened?" Travis asked.

"Sandy killed Dave," Anna said. "She was smuggling drugs in cupcakes, from the bakery to restaurants in Junction. Dave found out and wanted to tell you, and Sandy killed him." She shook her head, still dazed by all that had occurred. "I think she might have killed George Anton, too. She said the person who was supplying drugs to her had set up Anton to look like the person behind the whole thing, though he really didn't know anything."

"She tried to kill George, but he's alive," Lucas said. "He's on his way to the hospital, but I think he'll be okay."

"That's good." She covered her mouth with her hand, trying to hold back a sob. "Poor Dave. He really loved her, and she did that to him. She gave him dog tranquilizers then made him climb a ladder and put a noose around his neck. The way she talked about it was so...cold. And she faked those letters and shot the window out of the bakery herself."

Travis nodded. "She took advantage of the bakery's remote location, and she reckoned none of us would want to think a grieving widow could be responsible."

"Do you think you can stand?" Lucas asked.

She nodded and he helped her up.

"We'll need your statement," Travis said. "As soon as possible."

"Of course." She straightened. "I'm okay to talk about it." She turned to Lucas. "I didn't have food poisoning," she said. "Sandy doped one of the cupcakes she gave me. It was supposed to kill me, but I got sick before much of it could absorb into my system."

His expression looked grim. "We'll add that to the charges against her."

"Come on," Travis said. "You can tell us everything at the station. I'll meet you there."

He left and Lucas pulled her closer. "I'm so glad you're okay," he said and kissed her cheek.

She turned in his arms and kissed his mouth, hard and long, and not caring that the room was full of other people who were probably watching. "I'm glad I'm okay, too," she said when they finally broke apart. "I would have hated to die just when we had found each other."

"I can't even think about that." He stroked his thumb down her cheek. "I want to believe we have the rest of our lives to get to know each other."

Her breath caught at that vision. She had promised someone forever before and it hadn't worked out, but the thought of making that promise again didn't frighten her so much anymore. Maybe because this time she knew how fragile their time together could be, and it made her want to try harder not to let a moment slip away unnoticed. "Let's plan on it," she whispered.

GOING OVER EVERYTHING that had happened that afternoon took longer than the events themselves, Lucas realized after Travis finally switched off the recorder in the interview room and Anna signed her statement.

"Sandy Weiss isn't saying anything," Travis said. "But between your statement and George Anton's, plus the evidence we found at her home and at the bakery, she'll be charged with drug trafficking, murder and two counts of attempted murder."

"Why would she kill Dave?" Anna asked. "They

always seemed so happy together. I know she said he was upset about the drugs, but still."

"We'll search for the ladder she talked about," Travis said. "I'm hoping she'll tell us more, but it sounds like, after she gave Dave the phenobarbital, she was able to either persuade or force him to climb the ladder. Dave was a big guy, but she's stronger than most women. She used to compete in power-lifting competitions. Plus, he might have thought if he went along with her, he could talk her out of what she was doing. Until it was too late."

"She might have killed me if it hadn't been for Jacquie." Anna leaned down to pet the dog, who hadn't left her side since the ordeal had ended.

"I'm going to buy her a steak," Lucas said and leaned over to pet the dog, also.

"We're working with Junction law enforcement to track down the dealer who was supplying the drugs," Travis said. "The DA is still hopeful he can make a deal with Sandy to give them a name. It looks like she had a lot of money stashed in an overseas account, and we found a passport with her photograph and a different name, ready if she decided to leave the country. The sous-chef at Red Mesa, who Junction PD arrested, admitted to regularly retrieving drugs in the baked goods from Weiss Bakery. Apparently, every shipment included a box marked 'For Staff' and the drugs were hidden in plastic capsules in hollowed-out places in cakes and other pastries. We're also putting pressure on Darryl Singh to tell us who hired him to deliver that package to the bakery. I sent Gage out with Tony Meisner to retrieve the package from Singh's car. The box they brought back was full of fentanyl pills." He stood. "Thank you for your help, Anna. Lucas can take you home now."

"Are you ready to go?" Lucas asked when they were alone.

She met his gaze, her expression so weary but tender, too. "Can we go to your place?" she asked. "I'd like to see it."

"Of course." He stood and she rose, also, but instead of moving toward the door, she moved into his arms. He tightened his arms around her, wishing he could find the words to ease her distress. She would need more than words; she would need time, and he would give that to her.

"I couldn't believe Dave would kill himself, but I never would have thought Sandy would murder him," she said. "They seemed so much in love."

"Some people aren't capable of loving as much as others," he said. He rested his chin atop her head. "I used to think that about me. All Jenny wanted was for me to love her enough to commit to her for the rest of my life, and I couldn't do it."

"That doesn't make you a bad person," she said. "Not like Sandy. You were loyal to Jenny and did as much as you could for her. But marriage is a big commitment not everyone is ready to make."

"It is. But now I think that even though I couldn't make that promise to Jenny, I might be able to make it one day." He shifted so that he could look into her eyes. "To the right person."

"I know what you mean," she said. "One day. When the time is right."

"We don't have to rush," he said. "But I want us to be together."

"I want that, too." Her smile was shaky and her eyes glimmered with unshed tears. "I believe in you, Lucas. And that makes me believe in us."

"Yeah." He kissed her lightly, a seal on a promise, one he could make this time and keep. Forever.

* * * * *

Next month, look for another book in Cindi Myers's Eagle Mountain: Critical Response miniseries when Killer on Kestrel Trail *goes on sale!*

And if you missed the first title in the series, Deception at Dixon Pass *is available now, wherever Harlequin Intrigue books are sold!*

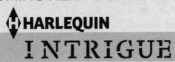

Get 3 FREE REWARDS!

We'll send you 2 FREE Books plus a FREE Mystery Gift.

FREE
Value Over
$20

Both the **Harlequin Intrigue®** and **Harlequin® Romantic Suspense** series feature compelling novels filled with heart-racing action-packed romance that will keep you on the edge of your seat.

YES! Please send me 2 FREE novels from the Harlequin Intrigue or Harlequin Romantic Suspense series and my FREE gift (gift is worth about $10 retail). After receiving them, if I don't wish to receive any more books, I can return the shipping statement marked "cancel." If I don't cancel, I will receive 6 brand-new Harlequin Intrigue Larger-Print books every month and be billed just $6.49 each in the U.S. or $6.99 each in Canada, a savings of at least 13% off the cover price, or 4 brand-new Harlequin Romantic Suspense books every month and be billed just $5.49 each in the U.S. or $6.24 each in Canada, a savings of at least 12% off the cover price. It's quite a bargain! Shipping and handling is just 50¢ per book in the U.S. and $1.25 per book in Canada.* I understand that accepting the 2 free books and gift places me under no obligation to buy anything. I can always return a shipment and cancel at any time by calling the number below. The free books and gift are mine to keep no matter what I decide.

Choose one:
- ☐ **Harlequin Intrigue Larger-Print** (199/399 BPA GRMX)
- ☐ **Harlequin Romantic Suspense** (240/340 BPA GRMX)
- ☐ **Or Try Both!** (199/399 & 240/340 BPA GRQD)

Name (please print)

Address — Apt. #

City — State/Province — Zip/Postal Code

Email: Please check this box ☐ if you would like to receive newsletters and promotional emails from Harlequin Enterprises ULC and its affiliates. You can unsubscribe anytime.

Mail to the **Harlequin Reader Service:**
IN U.S.A.: P.O. Box 1341, Buffalo, NY 14240-8531
IN CANADA: P.O. Box 603, Fort Erie, Ontario L2A 5X3

Want to try 2 free books from another series! Call 1-800-873-8635 or visit www.ReaderService.com.

*Terms and prices subject to change without notice. Prices do not include sales taxes, which will be charged (if applicable) based on your state or country of residence. Canadian residents will be charged applicable taxes. Offer not valid in Quebec. This offer is limited to one order per household. Books received may not be as shown. Not valid for current subscribers to the Harlequin Intrigue or Harlequin Romantic Suspense series. All orders subject to approval. Credit or debit balances in a customer's account(s) may be offset by any other outstanding balance owed by or to the customer. Please allow 4 to 6 weeks for delivery. Offer available while quantities last.

Your Privacy—Your information is being collected by Harlequin Enterprises ULC, operating as Harlequin Reader Service. For a complete summary of the information we collect, how we use this information and to whom it is disclosed, please visit our privacy notice located at corporate.harlequin.com/privacy-notice. From time to time we may also exchange your personal information with reputable third parties. If you wish to opt out of this sharing of your personal information, please visit readerservice.com/consumerchoice or call 1-800-873-8635. **Notice to California Residents**—Under California law, you have specific rights to control and access your data. For more information on these rights and how to exercise them, visit corporate.harlequin.com/california-privacy.

HIHRS23

HARLEQUIN
PLUS

Try the best multimedia subscription service for romance readers like you!

Read, Watch and Play.

Experience the easiest way to get the romance content you crave.

Start your **FREE TRIAL** at
www.harlequinplus.com/freetrial.